WISHES, DARES, & HOW TO STAND UP TO A BULLY

By Darlene Beck Jacobson

Creston Books

JACK

I jiggle the rod, trying
to interest a fish.
Pops expects some level of
ENTHUSIASM!!!

He gave up his day
to bring me here.

I wish the fish were biting
like last summer, he says.
We'd have caught a dozen by now.

In our bucket,
one sorry fish stares out.

If it was a fish that granted a wish
I'd ask it to bring
DAD home.

I wouldn't waste my wish on
another fish.

GONE

Dad's been gone almost a year.

At the start of fifth grade,
we tossed a ball after supper every night.
Then one night,
extra slices of pizza and
cupcakes with my favorite fudge frosting.
I should have known something was up.

We stayed outside after dark, laughing until my
teeth hurt, until he said,
I'm being sent overseas to do my job.

Isn't your job here with us?

When you're a soldier, you go
where your country needs you.

It won't be long, he said. I'll
be home for Christmas.

That was the only time
Dad ever told me
a lie.

Darlene Beck Jacobson

SORE

I ask Mom
what MIA, Missing In Action, means.

He's lost, she says.
He can't find his way back,
or they can't find him.

Her shoulders slump like mine when
Chip McCloskey hurls insults
at recess or at lunch.

Can't work
can't play
can't shake off words
that feel like a stick poking
an already sore spot.

Am I
MIA
too?

LOST

If I was lost
I'd look for something
anything
one familiar thing
to help me find my way. Why can't Dad
find his way?

Maybe he can't walk, but if he can crawl,
he can go somewhere,
find someone to help, right?

In Scouts they told us
you can look for signs when you're lost,
like moss growing on the north side of trees.

In one of Dad's letters he said
there were no paved highways or roads,
just dirt paths winding through a tangle of jungle.
Being in a place like that would make me forget
everything I learned about finding a way out.

If you speak another language,
how would anyone know you're lost,
even if you tried to tell them?
I got lost once in the grocery store. I cried,
and a nice old lady helped me find Mom.

If Dad cries
screams
yells
until his throat is sore, will anyone hear him?
Will anyone listen?
Will anyone help?

Darlene Beck Jacobson

LIAR

On the worst days
I think that MIA is
a liar's way of saying
Dad
is
probably
dead.

No one wants to say it,
that maybe he's dead,
so they make up a lie,
pretending everything might be fine.

Sometimes, when you tell a lie, repeat it
over and over again,
you start to believe it.
I tell myself
Dad isn't really lost.
He's hiding.
When you hide, you can
come out when things are safe,
when you're not afraid anymore.

When you're lost,
do you ever stop
being afraid?

MOON

President Kennedy said Americans are
in a race.
A space race to be
the first to land a man on the moon.

John Glenn, the hero astronaut,
went into space in a
rocketship named Friendship Seven.

In school they set up a TV,
and we watched the rocket blast off.
When it got into orbit, the whole school cheered.

When I think of it now, was John Glenn
worried
about getting lost somewhere in space?
If I had to be lost,
I'd want to be lost on earth.

Our teacher Mr. Metzger asked us if
we wanted to one day visit the moon.
All of us, the whole class, said yes.

I still say yes, but
only if my family and friends come with me.
Then if we got lost,
we'd be lost
together.

Darlene Beck Jacobson

LONG

Why does a day
feel so
L

O

N

G
when you hate what you're doing?

Mom says I need to help Gran and Pops.
Cut grass
paint fence posts
weed the garden and listen to boring stories.
They're letting us stay
all summer
L

O

N

G
I didn't ask to come here.
Mom wants to be around family,
Dad's family.
I like my grandparents.

It's just that I thought we three,
mom,
me,
and my sister Katy

were,
are
Dad's family.

MOVE

Mom thinks living with grandparents
all summer
will keep me busy, out of trouble.
Help us forget about
old things, learn
new things.

What things am I supposed to forget?
How our house still smells like Dad
when it rains?
How he hung the picture of the four of us
crooked on the living room wall?
How he could burp the Happy Birthday song?

Letters and phone calls stopped coming after
four months away. If we keep moving
we'll be too busy to worry, Mom says.

She never sits still.

When you're still,
you have to listen to the voice
in your head that thinks bad things.

I don't like that voice.
I guess I'd better
keep moving, too.

KATY

My sister makes me laugh
even when I feel like crying.

She spins in a circle,
pigtails swinging around
and around, until she falls drunk with dizziness,
a pile of laughter in the grass.

This time do it with me, Jack.
She grabs my hand. We twirl and spin.

Katy remembers Dad
in a little kid kind of way.
Not the staying up late to talk and sneak ice cream
when everyone else sleeps way.
If he came home,
he would be like a stranger.
Katy wouldn't grab
a stranger's hand and take him for a spin.

When we land in the grass,
a thought pokes me
like Katy does with her elbow
when I try to ignore her being a pest.

Will Dad someday seem like
a stranger to me, too?
How many spins does
it take to make
bad thoughts go away?

AWAY

When I talk about Dad to Katy,
she asks questions. A question machine,
asking and never answering.

When is he coming home?
Don't know, I say.
Why did he go away?
When you're a soldier,
it's your job to go away.

I try to say it like I believe it.
I don't like away, Katy says.
She makes a mad face,
really a sad face.

Being here means we're away
from home, I say.
We're with Gran and Pops, Katy says.
It's okay to be away when
we're all together.

Like going to the moon, I tell her.
What? she asks.
When they invent a ship
that takes people to the moon, we'll go together
because it's far away, I say.

Is Dad on the moon? she asks.
No, but he might as well be.

I wish Daddy's away was here, Katy sighs.
Me too, I say.

ASIA

Back home, at the house
we live in when we're not here,
there's a map on the wall next to my bed,
the whole world on a flat piece of paper.

After Dad put it up, we poked
pins with tiny green heads into
places we've been.

The pins are close together
in the eastern US because that's where we
always go on road trips and vacations.

There is one lonely pin
in California from when
we went to Disneyland before Katy
was born.

Before he left, Dad
pointed to a place farther away than
California, on the continent of Asia,
a place called Vietnam.

Put a pin there, Dad said,
so you'll always know
where I am.

Darlene Beck Jacobson

WEEK

It's been a week since we came to live
with Gran and Pops.
Seven bowls of cereal,
seven peanut butter-and-strawberry
jam sandwiches,
seven suppers with food
that looks funny on the small plates Gran uses.

Chicken drumsticks,
french-fries,
hot dogs, and meatloaf
taste like home.
Why do we have to eat so many vegetables?
Raw
cooked
hot
cold
they take up half the plate.

I check my ears in the mirror to make sure
I'm not turning into a rabbit.
Or should I check my teeth?

BIKE

I find a bike, a red Schwinn,
covered in cobwebs in Pops' shed.
One flat tire and the chain needs oil.

A polish with some of Pops' car wax
brings back the shine.

A Joe DiMaggio baseball card is clothespinned
to a spoke on the back wheel, like my bike
at home with a picture of
Mickey Mantle in the same place.

Can I ride it, Pops?
You bet, he says.
Your dad rode that bike everyday until
he got a car.

Pops chuckles when he tells me
the bike has a name,
Flash.
Todd rode like a Flash all over town.

I stare at Pops. He can't see me
because he's remembering,
watching Todd,
Dad,
ride Flash.

RIDE

I take Flash for a ride,
gliding through the air like
a warm knife glides
through butter. The seat
feels like my butt has been there before.

I pedal until my legs
are
on
fire.

Going everywhere
nowhere
anywhere
but here.

What would happen if I rode forever?
Would I stop thinking about Dad?

Would I stop missing our house
and the fort Dad helped me build
in the backyard?

If I rode backwards
ꓝꓷꓤAⱯꓔꓘƆA𐐒
Could I go back in time
to when everything was
boring
dumb
ordinary?

Why did I complain
when things were so good?

Why do I only miss something
once it's gone?

GIRL

I streak past a bike on the side of the road,
pink and purple streamers on
the handlebars. Where's
the girl who rides?

I stop, look around a field
filled with wildflowers.
In the middle, a girl as wild as a bird
spins
dances
jumps
through the tangle of blooms,
a fistful in one hand. She
stops
waves
shouts hello
as she runs up to me.

My name is Jill.
Jack, I say.
She giggles as she sings
that old rhyme that has our names.

When she's done singing, she
smiles and says, Don't
expect me to
tumble
crumble
or fumble.
I'm
not that kind of
girl.

TALK

Walking our bikes up the dusty road,
saying things you say
when you meet someone new.

Jill: Did you just move here?
Me: Living with my grandparents
for the summer.
Jill: The Sweet Shop has the best
milkshakes and candy.

Me: I like their pinball machines and comic books.
Jill: You can swim and fish at the lake.
Me: Fished once with Pops at a pond.
Jill: If you want to go sometime,
I know the best place for digging up night crawlers.
Maybe I'll see you there.

Me: Tomorrow?

She grins, stuffs the wildflowers
into the basket of her bike.
I watch her cloud of dust
until it disappears.

Maybe with
a friend
the summer without Dad can be
something
almost
bearable.

Darlene Beck Jacobson

JILL

Here's what I know about Jill.
She's eleven like me.
Crazy about bugs,
naming them like the scientists do.
Isn't afraid of putting a worm on a hook.

Her favorite color is pink.
She can make lemonade come out of her nose.
We never run out of things to talk about.
She makes me forget about Dad.
Almost
not really
but
she makes me laugh.

I catch a fish with one eye missing.
Jill says, Throw it back.
Why?
If it can survive like that,
it must have a special purpose,
don't you think?

I stare at the fish that doesn't look special,
wondering what happened to the other eye.
I'm naming it Fred, I say
before I throw it back.
Special things should have a name,
don't you think?

BALL

Katy is obsessed with a beach ball
Gran gave her to play with.
Names it Bouncy.
Bouncy rides in the car,
sits in an empty chair at the table,
Dad's chair.

She draws a face on the ball
with rainbow markers.
Looks nothing like Dad.

Here's what Bouncy can do, Katy demonstrates.
Bounce
roll
float
spin
sleep
blow air.
If Bouncy had legs, he could walk like me.
If Bouncy had arms, he could hold things like me.
Jack, can we make arms and legs for Bouncy?

Get a doll, I say.
A doll already looks like you.

Silly Jack,
a doll doesn't bounce and roll.

A ball isn't a substitute for Dad,
I tell her.

Darlene Beck Jacobson

GRAN

If Gran was a crayon,
she would be the green one.
She can grow vegetables on a rock
probably.

I help her pick vegetables from the garden
that takes up one corner of the yard.
Things I've never heard of.
Rutabaga
kohlrabi
parsnip
chard
leeks.
I think she's making up the names
until we have them
all together
in a soup one afternoon when it's cold and rainy.

Makes me wish for a cheeseburger
covered in
my favorite vegetable,
ketchup.

TAPE

Katy drags the sheet from her bed
onto the grass in the backyard.
Let's camp out, she says.

I tape one end to the fencepost
with Pops' duct tape.
Quack, quack, says Katy.
Why is it called duck tape, Jack?

I hold the roll up to her ear.
Listen.
Moooooo, I say.
It works the same for any animal, I tell her.

Then I'm calling it pig tape,
Katy squeals, and we take
turns making all the
barnyard sounds we can think of,
taping the other end of the sheet
to the picnic table.

Darlene Beck Jacobson

TENT

The sheet tent falls apart when it rains.
A soggy rag
hanging onto life by the sticky
wonder of pig tape.
It won't give up without
a tug of war.

Can you use pig tape
to hold a family together?

Pops finds a real tent
in the attic, big enough
for two kids pretending
to be somewhere they aren't.

Why are all the
cool things around here
covered in dust?

CAMP

Last summer before Dad left,
we went camping in the mountains.
Four of us squashed in a tent
smelling like sweat and bug spray.

Dad told ghost stories until
Mom begged him to stop
because I was afraid to leave the tent
to use the latrine.

We made flashlight shadow animals
with our fingers,
Katy clapping and begging for more.

Waking up to the
chirps
tweets
calls
of wild things we couldn't see,
roasting wieners on a stick for breakfast,
marshmallows at night.

Even the
corny songs Mom made us sing felt good.

Best
three
days
of
my
life
so
far.

Darlene Beck Jacobson

LOOK

Mostly
Jill and I meet each other
outside somewhere.

One day I ride past a house
on a street I never rode on before,
surprised to see a shiny truck and
two cars lined up across the yard.

All the other houses have only
one car or one truck.
Maybe this is the mayor's house,
the house of somebody $$ Rich $$.
Who else would have so many vehicles?

I stop looking when
Jill flies out the front door.
She has a can of worms and her pole.

What are you doing here, Jack?
How can her face look
surprised
embarrassed
worried
all at the same time?

I unstick my tongue.
I guess I'm going fishing with you.

I'll meet you at the pond, she says,
as I ride home to get my gear.

When I get to the pond a boy is there,

a trouble maker,
making trouble for Jill.

Darlene Beck Jacobson

MEAN

Tossing rocks into the water,
dumping her worms into the grass.

Stop it, Cody! Jill shouts.
He laughs and flicks her hair.

Why don't you leave her alone, I say.
He's shorter than me, so
I feel brave.

Cody turns his face to me,
making up for small
with loud and wild.

Who are you to tell me what to do?
He bounces a rock off my shoulder.

She's my sister.
I rule this town.
Don't forget it.
A sneer and a smirk,
he hops on Jill's bike and rides away.

How can a girl with a laughing face and
orange freckles on her nose
be related to a kid like that?
Why is he so mean to his own sister?

LILY

Mom makes us write letters every week,
sending them to the old address we have
for Dad.

Katy draws people with
arms
legs
hair
coming out of
a big circle.

I tell Dad the stuff we're doing.
Mom says we should write
happy
cheerful
positive things
so Dad knows we are fine.

Mom signs each letter with
XXX
OOO
and a doodle of a
flower that looks like a
Lily,
her name.

FINE

Is it lying
to tell Dad we're fine when
we're just pretending?

Maybe it's only me pretending to be fine.
It's what Mom expects.

But when I watch Gran, when
she's not looking,
her forehead wrinkles
eyes crinkle
hand shakes
never completely still.

Pops spends so much time
polishing
arranging
re-arranging
tools in the workshop.
Not his tools, the ones Dad left behind.

And then there's Mom,
filling every quiet minute and empty space with
movement, snapping pictures of us
with her new Instamatic camera.

Roll after roll of film
sit in a box on the nightstand,
waiting to be developed.
Waiting for Dad.

Katy is really the only one

who is fine.
She doesn't know any better.

BAKE

During the school year Mom
teaches second grade at our elementary school,
walking with me to work while Katy stays
with Mrs. Nunzio, our neighbor.

During the summer Mom usually
stays home with us.
That's what she did when Dad was around.

Here Mom gets a part time job at a bakery.
Leaves before we wake up some mornings
and comes back after lunch,
smelling like donuts and cinnamon.

We get to try yesterday's treats,
the ones that nobody wanted
to buy.
Chocolate éclairs
apple turnovers
cream puffs
crumb buns
brownies with walnuts
smell wonderful
taste good
even when they're leftover.

Even though Gran protests,
we have a dessert-for-supper day
with NO VEGETABLES.

So far it's the best supper
since we've been here.

BITE

For the county fair one summer,
Mom baked a blueberry pie.
It won a red ribbon,
second place.

Let's celebrate, said Dad.
Who can take the biggest bite
without using a fork?
Hands behind your back.

Me
Mom
Dad
three-year-old Katy with
heads touching as we hovered over the pie.
One, two, three, go!

Dove in and came up with
purple chin and crust crumbs on my face.
Mom and Katy too.
Dad's face was clean.
Why didn't you take a bite? I asked.

Didn't want to miss seeing you three dive in.
No manners at all.
Shameful
shocking.
Dad's smile a mile wide,
laughter filling his mouth instead of pie.

Mom made him take his turn
while we three watched,
laughing as he

snorted his way through a bite.
My silly drawing of us
with four purple faces
hangs on my bedroom wall.

COMICS

Pops gives me a quarter
so I can have some fun
at the Sweet Shop.

I check out the comic book rack
for the new Spiderman or Superman.
Nothing new.
A game of pinball would be okay, but
two kids are at the machine.
I look over the candy in the glass case,
maybe a Snickers or a big Tootsie Roll?

The pinball game must be over, there's
shouting and cheering.
When I make my way back, I recognize
one of the boys,
the one making the most noise,
bragging about winning,
beating the other boy at the game.

Jill's brother Cody pushes past me,
gives me a shove,
not caring that there are
grown-ups
sitting at the counter, sipping coffee,
watching everything.

Get out of my way, he says,
shoving again. This time he
tips over the rack of comic books,
laughing, as both of them scurry to the door,
like rats escaping a storm.

Darlene Beck Jacobson

Mr. Belcher, the owner, shakes his head, telling them
instead of yelling at them,
Don't come back here again.

He gives me a free ice cream soda
and a comic book for helping him
clean up the mess.

Helping him seems
like a good idea since
his left arm
and hand
don't seem to work right.

I save the quarter for another day.

PALS

The next day I
ride past the house where I saw Jill,
thinking maybe she wants to hang out.
She sits on a front step,
picking at a scab on her knee.

Want to go to the
Sweet Shop? I say. We can
both have a soda with
the quarter Pops gave me.

Jill frowns, says,
Every time I go there,
Cody shows up and makes trouble.

He can't go back. I tell her about what
happened yesterday. Mr. Belcher
likes me. We'll be okay.

We hang out all afternoon and
Mr. Belcher tells us we're welcome anytime.
When we get back on our bikes and
turn the corner,
Cody is waiting for us.

Darlene Beck Jacobson

DUMB

Cody runs in front of us,
thinking
hoping
figuring we'll stop.
Only a dumb person would stop
if they saw a kid growling like a bear
coming after them.

Jill swerves her bike out of his way.
I try to do the same, but
he lunges for me,
yanks my shirt until I topple onto the road,
my fists still hanging onto the handlebars,
heart thumping in my ears,
feeling dumb laying in the dirt.

Jill screams loud enough
so everyone in the street looks over.

Cody laughs his hyena laugh as he
runs away, kicking up a cloud of dust
that settles on me.

As I pick myself up
and spit dust from my mouth,
Jill comes over and says,
Sometimes I wish my brother
would disappear.

HIDE

Cody doesn't like me hanging out with Jill.
He and another boy, Brad,
constantly chase us, making trouble.

Call me a sissy because
I'd rather hang out with
a girl
than be part of the mess
they make.

Breaking windows
running through gardens
crushing flowers
dumping trashcans
picking on little kids.
Why can't they find something
useful to do? Is this
their idea of fun?

We look for places to hide,
in a cornfield
in an old shed
under a train bridge.

Our best hiding spot is
up in a tree.
We watch them from the tallest branch.

When they get tired of looking,
we shimmy down the tree,
smiling.

Darlene Beck Jacobson

PEST

I ask Mom if Jill can camp out
in the tent with me and Katy.

She looks at me with
surprised eyebrows and smiling eyes,
wanting to know about Jill.

We fish together sometimes
and she likes bugs and
does tricks on her bike, I say.
She needs a break from her brother.

He's a pest, I say
because
Mom would be mad at me
if I called him something worse.

You think Katy's a pest sometimes, Mom says.

She's only a little pest.
Jill's brother is
a
BIG
HUGE
GIANT
ENORMOUS
GARGANTUAN
pest.

I think we need to meet Jill,
Mom says.

MEET

I guess Jill passes the test
you can't study for, the one
where you meet your friend's family
for the first time.

You can tell by the looks on their faces
if people are happy or not.
Not just a
smile-on-the-face happy,
but the way everyone
stands, relaxed and doing
what they always do,
without being like robots.

Gran
Pops
Mom
Katy
stare with sunbeam faces
when they meet Jill.

Darlene Beck Jacobson

HUGE

Katy makes a huge deal
out of the campout with Jill.

For me getting ready is
putting a sleeping bag and pillow in
the tent with
a flashlight, canteen of water.

Katy packs like she might be gone for a week,
stuffed animals
every sock she owns
her favorite books
Bouncy.
All stuffed into the tent that seemed big enough
but now looks like it might explode!
It's one night, I say.

This is what I need for one night, Jack.

Where will Jill put her sleeping bag? I ask.

Katy pats a skinny spot next to
the wall of the tent.
Right here, next to me. She beams
like her face is made up of
lightening bug butts.

The idea of a sister,
even a borrowed one,
is too much for a
little kid to hold inside.

PINK

Katy vibrates with excitement,
all three of us in the tent.
There is so much pink,
I feel like I'm stuck
inside a cotton candy machine.

We catch lightning bugs
and take Bouncy for a hop in the dark.
Jill ties fancy knots like sailors do
and has a pocket knife like the one Dad
gave me.

She shows us how to blow a whistle,
a blade of grass pressed between our thumbs.
I teach her how to finger snap.
We don't stop until our fingers get sore.

We take turns reading Katy's favorite books,
making goofy voices for the characters,
until Katy yawns and closes her eyes.

SAFE

After Katy falls asleep,
Jill asks me where is the place
I feel most safe.

Stuffed in our sleeping bags,
staring at the tent ceiling,
my mouth glued shut
because I don't know if there is
such a place.

Home felt safe before.
You first, I say.

She's quiet a
long time, like maybe
she's fallen
asleep.

BEST

Then Jill tells me a story.

When Cody was eight and I was seven,
we were best friends, like you and Katy.
Dad and Mom started fighting
when they thought we were sleeping.
Saying mean things to each other
until one day Dad left.

Mom didn't know what to do.

She went out sometimes and we
stayed home with a babysitter.
Cody tried to act brave and tough,
saying we didn't need a babysitter
or anyone else.

One day Mom came home with Dale.
Dale bought us candy and
took us bowling, acting like
he was our new dad.

Mom liked having him around.
She didn't have to worry about what to do.
Pretty soon he was our new dad. Then
there was no more nice.
He ignored me but not Cody.

Jill breathes in and out,
making the cool night air suddenly warm.

I used to think being
a favorite was the best thing.

Darlene Beck Jacobson

For Cody
it was the worst.

TOP DOG

Dale expected Cody to be Top Dog.
Be the best or be a loser, Dale said.
No room for a loser
around here.

Dale set up contests for everything
between him and Cody.
Beat me, Cody, he'd say.
Cody liked
attention
competition.
When the games were simple,
it was fun, easy to win.

Dale kept score.
Too many losses and he took things away.
Dessert
catcher's mitt
bike.

To get them back, Cody had to beat Dale.
When he couldn't do that, he blamed
me
Mom
everyone else, except Dale.

Mom spends her time keeping
Dale happy.
She doesn't seem to notice
that Cody is different.
He's Top Dog now.
Number One Bully.

Darlene Beck Jacobson

ACHE

Jill forgets to ask me about
my safe place. I'm glad
because if I start talking about Dad,
I might never stop.

When Jill runs out of words,
she closes her eyes, snores.

I lay awake with a new ache
next to the one Dad made when
he went away.
It comes from knowing
bullies aren't born. They're made.

Can they be unmade?

I think about how having a Dad who's
missing is the
awful
terrible
worst thing for me.

For some kids, like Jill and Cody,
having no dad
might be
the best thing.

DARK

When I was Katy's age, I used to be
afraid of the dark.
Shadows on the wall from cars passing by,
flashing headlights
sounds of the night
made me bury my face under the covers.

I imagined all the scary things I couldn't see,
hiding
lurking
waiting to get me
if I wasn't watchful. One night
I woke up crying from a nightmare,
screaming for the monsters to go away.

Mom and Dad rushed into the room. Dad pulled
me onto his lap, rocking me
until I stopped crying.

He asked me where
the scary places were. As I pointed out each one,
he pointed a flashlight beam on it.
This is what it looks like
in the light, he said. No matter how many times
we turn off the light, it doesn't change. He
handed the light to me and
told me to shine it wherever I thought
the scary things were. I moved the beam in all
the corners
under the bed
inside the closet
behind the door
flicking it on and off until I was satisfied.

Darlene Beck Jacobson

Then Dad said,
Remember in the dark what you learned in the light.

The dark doesn't scare me anymore,
but sometimes,
times like this,
it makes me sad.

TRIP

I don't see Jill after the campout.
Her family goes on a trip to visit cousins
six hours away.
Jill didn't want to go,
but Dale said she had to.

I feel sorry for her,
sitting in a car for six hours
with two bullies and
a mom who is maybe too happy
in a fake happy way
to see that her kids aren't
fake happy or any
kind of happy.

Things are different here with Gran and Pops,
but at least Mom
is the same Mom she always was,
mostly. And she's
the first one to notice
when one of us is acting weird.

Darlene Beck Jacobson

WAIT

Can't sit around everyday for a week,
waiting for Jill to come back from her trip.
Sleeping in the tent with Katy and
her dumb ball
is
no
fun.

I never
hardly ever
get to pick
what we watch on TV.

Katy bugs me to take her fishing.
Gran packs peanut butter and strawberry jam
sandwiches, some grapes
and a thermos of lemonade.

Katy wiggles onto the handlebars of the bike
and we head out to the pond for her
first fishing lesson.

FISH

Katy feels sorry for worms
and won't fish with them.
I make balls of dough
from the crusts of our sandwiches to
bait her hook.

She breaks every rule about fishing.
Making loud noises, scaring the fish.
She can't stand in one spot
more than a minute without
dancing
wiggling
spinning
tangling the fishing line
asking so many questions
my ears are ready to
EXPLODE!!!

When are we going to catch a
FISH!!!? she shouts for the
tenth time, dropping her pole to
chase a butterfly.

Fish don't come around when it's noisy,
so zzzzip your lips, I say.

She pretends to zip her lips,
humming the tune to
"Twinkle, Twinkle, Little Star."
Good
grief.

Darlene Beck Jacobson

FRED

After lunch I'm ready to leave.
No fish today, let's go, I say.

Maybe the fish don't like worms.
Maybe they're veterinarians, Katy says.
She means vegetarians because
she hands me a grape and says
put it on the hook, Jack, please?

Can you sit without making a sound,
quiet as a stone?
She puts a finger to her lips, Shhhhh.

I hook the grape, toss the line,
hand the rod to Katy.
Before I settle onto the grass,
the line gives a tug.
Too heavy for me, I can't do it, Jack.

I grab the rod and pull a fish out,
a fish with one eye.
It's Fred, I tell her.

Katy strokes Fred's tail with a pinkie.
A special fish, I say.
Like magic special?
Katy's two eyes as wide as Fred's one.
Don't know, I say.

Katy frowns, so I say,
make a wish, quick before Fred goes back.

Pancakes for supper! she wishes,

kissing Fred on the tail.
Pancakes, I agree. As I slip
Fred into the water, he seems to
wink his eye before he swims away.

Darlene Beck Jacobson

TRUE

It's true, it's true,
Katy sings when we sit down to eat
towers of pancakes stacked on plates,
waiting for butter and syrup.

What's true? Mom asks.
Fred
Is
Magic.
Katy says each word,
licking syrup off a spoon,
eyes closed like she is having the
best
day
ever.

As I tell them about the one-eyed
fish and Katy's wish, can they hear
my heart banging? Do they see
the zinging jolts of electricity
running through me?

Gran smiles and says,
I woke up wondering what to cook
for supper today, and right after lunch
a little voice in my head
told me to make pancakes.
Isn't that funny?

Funny, says Pops.
Funny, agrees Mom.

There's something

funny
strange
weird
that makes me wonder,
did Fred the one-eyed fish
grant Katy's wish?

And if he did,
do I
can I
why shouldn't I
make a wish?

The only wish worth wishing.

First I need to find out
how this wishing thing works.

Darlene Beck Jacobson

POPS

Pops is a plumber.
Leaky pipes
busted toilets
clogged sinks
keep him making house calls all day
and sometimes at night. A doctor
for sick pipes.

I go with him on one call
to fix a washing machine,
handing him tools, holding a flashlight
while he takes out an old part, puts in a new one.

Talking about baseball is okay.
Talking about fishing
makes me remember the wish and
wonder if it really happened.

Did Gran ever make pancakes for supper before? I ask.
Not as long as we've been married, Pops says.
Can a fish make a wish come true?

Pops smiles and says,
If you want something bad enough,
when it happens
you'll believe just about anything.

How else can you explain
something that's never happened before? I ask.
Pops chuckles. Sometimes a mystery
isn't meant to be solved, only to be enjoyed.

What if you could have a wish? I ask.

What would you wish for?

He looks at me a long minute.
Same thing you'd wish for, he says, neither of us
needing to say it out loud.

Darlene Beck Jacobson

MISS

We stop at Pops' favorite diner
after the plumbing job is done.
Men need a treat after hard work, he says.
Apple pie for Pops,
chocolate brownie with a scoop of
chocolate ice cream for me.

Todd's favorite dessert, Pops says.
Watching you eat is like watching him eat
when he was your age.

Having you all with us
keeps our hope from sinking
and fading away, says Pops.

He sniffs, like he's got something in his nose.
You and Katy are the best parts of him,
you know? Pops pats my shoulder.

I wish I had more milk
to wash down the last bite of brownie,
because it's stuck
in my throat.

DRAW

A box of chalk is what it takes
to get Katy to stop asking me
to take her to see Fred,
so she can make another wish.

Even though I'm
itching
twitching
longing to ask a fish, ask Fred
to bring Dad back home,
we draw a hopscotch board and
every animal I can think of
up and down the sidewalk in front of the house.

Katy colors them in with rainbow chalk while I
think about Fred and if it really happened.

Mom says it was a coincidence.
Probably it was,
but in case it wasn't,
I don't want Katy asking for dumb things
if I catch Fred again.

How many times do you wish for things,
dumb
stupid
useless things
not realizing you're wishing?

If I'm going to wish Dad home,
maybe I should learn a little more about
what happens when you wish for
something more

Darlene Beck Jacobson

than pancakes.

Maybe I need some proof
that wishes can come true.

TALE

I go to the library and ask for stories about
wishing and if wishes in the stories
come true.
The librarian shows me a tale called
The Fisherman and His Wife,
a story where a fish grants wishes.

Even though the wife made the fisherman
ask for things, he had to do the asking and
only had three wishes. The wishes
didn't make them happy, because
they didn't turn out the way they thought.

The wishes backfired because you have to make
the wish using the
right
careful
exact words.

My wish isn't for
power
fame
fortune.
It's a wish to bring Dad home.

What could be more right than
that wish?

My whole body tingles with excitement, ready
to make my wish. The only wish
worth making.

Until

Darlene Beck Jacobson

I read the second tale called
The Monkey's Paw.
A man and woman ask
the monkey's paw for some money.
The next day their only son
has an accident,
gets mangled in a machine and
dies.

They receive his life insurance money,
the exact amount they asked for.
The man wants to get rid of the paw,
but the woman misses her son
so much, she uses a wish,
asking to bring her dead son back.

When they hear a knock on the door,
the man knows it's his dead son who is
probably messed up,
bloody
like a zombie
knocking and knocking.

Before his wife runs to open the door,
he uses his last wish to
send his son back to where he came from.

By the time I finish reading,
hairs on my arms and spine
are standing straight up like soldiers.

I would scream! except
you're supposed to be quiet
in a library.

What if that

or something else
bad
horrible
worse
happens
when I wish Dad home?

The words you use in a wish
REALLY
ABSOLUTELY
POSITIVELY
have to be the right ones,
otherwise anything
something
the worst unthinkable thing
might happen.

I need to think about this wish and
maybe see what Jill thinks about it too.

BUSY

I keep Katy so busy,
she forgets all about Fred.

Trips to the playground,
ice cream sodas, blowing soap bubbles
until we're dizzy.
We even make sandcastles at a
pretend beach sand pile
behind the garage where Pops
keeps his plumbing supplies.

Dressed in swimsuits and snorkels,
Mom takes us to a lake Sunday afternoon.
It's bigger than our fishing pond where there's a
No Swimming sign, and
we stay all day
looking underwater for
snails
fish
pretty rocks.

I find a quarter and a dime.
Katy finds a rusty charm bracelet
which makes us act like pirates.

Even Mom says things like
shiver me timbers
arrggghh
ahoy, matey
until she makes us walk the plank
back to the car to go home.

Is it okay

to have a good day,
one of the best days,
without even thinking
once
about Dad?

Darlene Beck Jacobson

BACK

Jill comes back tomorrow. First thing
I'm going to find the quietest
safest place to talk about Fred,
my plan for a wish,
and see what Jill thinks.

We'll go up into the big oak tree
at the end of Pops' street.
Hidden from nosy eyes and ears.
No one bothers us there.
Maybe we can decide what to do.

How
should I wish Dad home? Or should I wish
for something else? A practice wish first?

Having two wishes is
getting heavy to carry around
alone.
Will Jill know what to do?

HARD

Fishing is the only sport that feels
okay doing it alone. You don't have to
worry about catching something.

It's hard to spend a day not fishing,
especially when I have no one to
do something
nothing with.
Hard to wait until Jill gets back
to help me decide
how to use the wishes.

A thing as important as a wish coming true
shouldn't be rushed.
Something hard to do seems easier when you don't
think about it.

How do you stop thinking
about something that can change your life?

The more I try to stop
thinking about the wish,
the more I think about
Dad. The more I miss him.

The more I want him
to be here.

Darlene Beck Jacobson

NEED

We need to get as far away from Cody
as possible, is the first thing Jill says
when I see her riding her bike
outside Gran's house.

Was the trip really bad? I ask.

No, the trip was really good, and Cody was
the old Cody
because we were with our older cousins.
There was no one to show off for,
no one to bully.

Dale did the showing off,
bragging to mom's family who'd never met him
and don't know what he's like.
He ignored Cody all week.

On the ride home, I told Cody I liked
spending the week with him, like before.
Cody smiled, whispered in my ear,
Got lots to make up for when we get back.
Tell your boyfriend to watch out.
I told him you're not my boyfriend.

Then he called you my girlfriend.
I called him a jerk which made him act like one
again, even more.
I made a promise to stop talking to Cody.

Let's go somewhere where we can talk, I say.
I need to tell you something
you're never going to believe.

TREE

We hide our bikes in the bushes, then
climb to the top branch of our favorite tree
where we can see anyone who comes close,
but they can't see us through all the leaves.

For a
L
O
N
G
time we don't say anything,
like we forgot how to talk.

I listen to
leaves brushing against
each other and my heart beating like it's
in my head. A thumping so loud,
everyone must hear it.

Jill breathes fast next to me.
Her hair smells like coconut,
and the freckles on her nose
are darker than I remember.

She pokes me with an elbow and says,
Okay, I'm ready to forget trouble
dressed up like Cody because I want to know
what happened here.

What makes you forget how to talk?
Her eyes are so wide.
Tell me, she says.

Darlene Beck Jacobson

BELIEVE

We straddle the tree branch, face to face.
I need to see her face when I say this.

Jill listens to the story about Fred,
staring at me, her mouth an "O."
She doesn't even blink, so I
know she believes me.

Two more wishes, I say.
And the big one I want to make might
not turn out
the way I want it to.
What would you do? I ask.

Jill frowns and points a finger in the air.
Katy made the wish, Jill says.
She gets two more
and then someone new gets a turn.
You get three of your own, right?

Maybe,
except I was the one who caught the fish,
like in the story. A fisherman only gets
three so there are two left, right?

There's one way to find out, Jill whispers.

PLAN

Tomorrow we go
to the fishing spot and
I will
try to catch Fred, Jill says.
When I do, I'll make a wish
and we'll see if it comes true.

What if I catch him? I say.

Maybe you can just watch
to make sure you don't catch Fred again.
We can see if Fred grants wishes
to anyone who catches him.

It's a good plan, I say as we
scurry down the tree.
Maybe a practice wish
will help me decide
if my wish
is
can be
might be
the right one to make.

TEST

We leave the house early, before breakfast,
before Katy wakes up and
asks millions of questions,
before Cody wakes up and follows us.

I bring two bananas to eat,
grapes to bait the hook
in case the worms don't work.

While we wait for Fred
I ask Jill, What are you going to wish for?

I thought all night about my wish, Jill says.
It shouldn't be a dumb one,
just in case.
She looks at me to see if I agree,
and I feel like a big,
heavy worry just disappeared.

The wish should make a difference,
even if it's just a test, I say.

Jill nods and says, I'm going to ask Fred
to make Cody stop
bothering us.

SAME

We go to the same spot where
I caught Fred both times before,
sitting on the bank next to each other.
Even the sunshine and insects buzzing
feel the same.

Jill puts a worm on the hook
and throws her line
into the pond, staring at me with the
same stare from up in the tree.
We cross fingers and cross eyes, giggling
while we wait for Fred.

We eat the bananas, making
monkey faces at each other.
Laughing makes me nervous,
like I'm taking a test I never
studied for and don't know the answers to.

Will it be better or worse
if we fail this test?
Will passing
this test mean I can make
my Dad wish?

Darlene Beck Jacobson

CODY

I hear them and then
I see them coming across the field,
Cody and Brad, shouting and
hurling insults at
each other, until they find us,
sitting, waiting for a fish
our fish
the fish
waiting for Fred.

You losers can't even catch a fish. Cody
flings the net into the water.

Jill stares at the spot, lips clamped shut as
a ripple spreads out toward us, the net
floating across the pond
like an empty raft.

I keep my eyes on
Cody, who grabs grapes,
shoves them into his
mouth, daring me to stop him.
He reaches for the can of worms.

Jill stares so hard at the water,
trying to keep her promise to
not talk to Cody,
trying so hard to ignore the
loudest thing.

I jump up and snatch the can
of worms before he does.

He stops, stares frozen for a minute,
long enough for me to
collect my courage.

PUSH

Things you push:
buttons
doorbells
snowballs
swings
a wagon, which you can also pull.

Most of the things you push
move, give way a little,
loosen up with the pushing.

When one kid tries
to push another with
hands or words,
a kid can
move
give in
or stand tall

and refuse to take a push as the
final answer.

When Cody tries to push,
I figure the best thing for me to do
is take root, stay put
because sometimes
it takes more than a
push
to make something or someone,
to make me,
move.

STEP

I take a step toward Cody.
He steps away, shouting to his friend.
Not much of a friend,
who laughs and mostly ignores him.

Brad looking for his own way
to bully, pitching rocks
into the pond, right next to where Jill fishes.

Another step forward for me,
one step back for Cody,
mad on his face, in his eyes.

Instead of a bully team
of two, it's just
Cody and me, staring and stepping.

He takes one baby step in my direction,
me just standing,
heart racing but staring anyway, until
Jill shouts, I've got him, Jack!

I don't have to look
to know
she caught Fred.

Darlene Beck Jacobson

YELL

I step away from Cody, step back to Jill,
her mouth open wide.

It isn't a whisper
but a YELL, a shout so loud
even Katy could probably
hear it back at Gran's house.

**I
WISH
CODY
WOULD
LEAVE US
ALONE
!!!!!**

She looks at Fred, then at me, before the fish
wiggles free from her hand,
disappearing into the water.

By the time I realize Jill made her wish,
Cody and Brad
are gone.

TIME

It feels like a
long time and no time
before we look at each other and
breathe again.

Where did they go? Jill whispers,
staring at the water as if
she expects Cody to come
jumping out like a porpoise.

The pond is so still, even
the net has stopped drifting,
stuck in the middle of the water,
waiting for rescue.

Birds sing
crickets chirp
insects buzz
blades of grass rustle
in the breeze.

The only human noise is
our breathing and heartbeats
which sound like
cannon booms
to me.

Darlene Beck Jacobson

SLOW

We walk back to our bikes
real slow,
not speaking.
Like the whole world has stopped
and if we move
too fast
we might
miss something.

I expect Cody to
be behind every bush,
ready to jump out
at us and be
like he always is.

But
when we get to our bikes,
we are alone.

The kind of alone that
makes me wonder,
where did everyone go?
Are we the only
two left?

FREE

I close my eyes, count to ten, then
open them again, expecting it all
to be a dream.

Does this mean my wish...? Jill asks
...Your wish, I say, Came true.
Cody won't bother us anymore.
We're free.

Jill sighs so long and hard, I think
she might blow away like
a balloon
when you let out the air.

She spins in a circle
like Katy does until
she falls onto the grass.
She stares up at me, squinting
into the sun.

What will it be like,
not having to hide from Cody
anymore? We can do
what we want, she says.
And we each
have two wishes left.

Darlene Beck Jacobson

GOOD

Riding all over town
to the places we like to go,
and everywhere
we have each place to ourselves.
No one bothers or chases us away.

Just the sound of our bikes in the wind,
baseball card flapping
clapping
snapping on the spokes.

No talking because
we don't want to break the spell,
undo the wish,
turn something good
into something bad.

For the first time since I met Jill,
she is still.
Only her legs pump the pedals
of the bike.

Before the
wish, every inch of her
twitched
jumped
swiveled
always watching behind.

Now she stares straight ahead,
like that thingy on a ship
pointing the way forward.

HERE

We stop first at
Jill's house. It looks the same.
One car missing, so Dale must be
at work.

Wait here a minute. Jill runs into the house.
I stay on my bike, not believing Cody
won't take it
if I'm not careful.

Other kids play
in other yards, dogs bark, a car drives by.
It's Mr. Belcher from the
Sweet Shop. I wave.
He keeps driving like he doesn't see me.

Jill runs up to me, frowns.
Mom is sleeping. I tried to wake her up, but
when she opened her eyes she called me
Cody, like she didn't know it was me.

How about Cody? I ask.

She shakes her head.
I can't find him, she says.

Darlene Beck Jacobson

INVISIBLE

Jill shouts to the kids across the street.
We see them, hear them,
all the noises they make are
loud and clear, but
no one answers when we yell,
like they can't
see us
hear us.

We are invisible.

I have to check my house, I say,
wanting to get away,
far away, from this strange
thing.

We need to stay together in case…

I don't hear the rest of what Jill says
because
I'm riding fast, trying
to stop thinking about how
Jill's wish
has gone wrong.

DEAF

They are here doing
what they do. Mom
in the kitchen making lunch.
Gran in her garden. Pops is
at work
probably, so that's not weird.

What's weird is,
they don't see us or
hear us or even
feel us moving around.

I give Mom a kiss on the cheek.
She stops spreading mustard on bread,
frowns a bit
flicks hair off her face,
calls for Katy.

Katy. Where is she?
We rush to the tent in the
backyard, and there she is
with Cody and Brad.
They're tossing Bouncy while Katy cries,
begs them to give Bouncy back.

STOP IT, CODY!!! Jill shouts.
I try to grab the ball.
It slips past my hands on the way to Brad.

I yell so hard my throat
hurts. No one looks
at us, no one hears us.
Everyone is blind and deaf.

Darlene Beck Jacobson

Jack and Jill
alone.

JOKE

I shut my eyes tight,
doing what I do to fall asleep
or when I'm scared.

I count backward from
one hundred to one, breathing in
and out with each number.
Mostly, I only get to fifty or forty before
I fall asleep, but now
I reach one.

I open my eyes, imagining this is all
a bad joke.
Ha, ha, Jack
Ha, ha, Jill, we got you good.

Then I see Katy holding Bouncy,
squashed flat, torn, and
not bouncing anymore.

How could anyone
play a joke
this mean?

Darlene Beck Jacobson

WRONG

We have to go back and catch
Fred, I say. Something
went wrong
with your wish.

Jill looks
confused
worried
angry
all at once.
I don't understand, she says.

Why is this happening?
I wished that Cody would
stop bothering us. She
rubs a hand over her eyes,
watching Katy
run into the house crying,
Cody and Brad laughing as they
kick a rusted can down the street.

No, you didn't, I say
because now I know
what happened to the wish.
You said, I wish Cody would
leave us alone.

The wish came true just
the way you said it.

We are alone and we
have to go back to Fred
and make a new wish.

MESS

We have to undo the
mess, the wish that
went wrong.
Make things the way
they used to be, I say.

With Cody bothering us? Jill asks.

At least then he wasn't picking
on Katy, I say.
If everything goes back
to the way it was before, then
we can use
your last wish to get it right.

Jill finally agrees and we ride to
the pond as if
our bikes had wings.

Darlene Beck Jacobson

CAN'T

A forever morning,
eternity afternoon,
sitting
waiting
wondering why we can't catch
a fish,
any fish
the only fish we want,
need, to catch.

Calling Fred in our loudest voices,
as if that would work better
than a worm on a hook.

What if we never catch Fred again? Jill's voice
a croaking sound that turns
my skin goose-bumpy, pools in her eyes
spilling over with tears.

Never being seen by anyone, my
family forgetting me,
never getting a chance to maybe
use my own wishes,
my Dad wishes,
makes me squeeze my own eyes shut.

How will we ever fix this?
Where are you Fred? I whisper.
A prayer:
We really messed up the last wish.
We need you.

As I wipe my eyes and open them,

the line gives a
small jiggle,
whispering back.

UNDO

We both stare at
Fred as he sits in Jill's hand,
blinking that eye, that one cold
fish eye.

Go on, I say, Fred is waiting.
Slowly and carefully
this time, because we can't make a mistake.

Jill says, I wish
everything was back the way it was
before
I made the other wish.

She looks at me. I nod.
That's the wish I want, Fred, she says.

Fred winks his moldy old fish eye and
slithers back under the water.

We go, separately,
to our own houses to see
if this wish
came true.

WHEW

Mom asks me where
I've been all morning
when I get back. She messes up
my hair like she always does when
she wants me to comb it.

Gran brings a basketful of
vegetables from the garden
and sets it on the table.

Would you help me can
some of these today, Jack? she asks.

Sure, I say
because doing even that boring thing,
that vegetable thing,
makes me feel relief, like you feel after
you find out your worst
worry was not so bad.

The best relief is when Katy
asks me to play with her after lunch. As we sit
around the table, I blow
a big cloud
of relief, feeling light, almost floating.

Whew.

Darlene Beck Jacobson

PINKY-SWEAR

We're out in the tent without Jill,
because I need
some time away from wishing
and fishing, and I'm afraid if I
see Jill, my relief will
disappear like we did. Sort of.

Katy wants to play house,
furry critters side-by-side around the tent
in a circle, a wooden box
in the center set as a table, filled with
Katy-size cups, saucers, and a plastic tea pot.

As I drink water tea,
munch stale crackers spread with jam,
I ask Katy if anything
something
one funny thing
happened to her today,
this morning before lunch.

I had a dream, Jack. Part of it was scary.
A boy stole Bouncy and
poked holes in him. He made me cry.
Know what was funny, Jack?
No, I say, my skin suddenly prickly.

When the boy was mean to me and Bouncy,
I forgot you were my brother.
I didn't even know I had
a brother, isn't that funny?

No, that's the

scary part of your dream, I say.
I don't ever want you to forget
I am your brother, promise?

We pinky-swear to
be sure the promise sticks like pig tape.

Darlene Beck Jacobson

FLAT

In the middle of the tea party, Katy says,
There is something wrong
with Bouncy, Jack. He
stopped bouncing and
he's losing weight.

I want to laugh because
it's a silly thing to imagine
a ball losing weight when
it really just needs air.

The look on Katy's face stops me.

She brings it out from
under her sleeping bag,
flat, like it was run over or stomped.
What happened? I ask.

Katy's shoulders go
up and down, head side to side.
Maybe I bounced him too hard, or
was my dream real? The mean boy part,
not the I don't have a brother part?

Just like that, relief
disappears and the feeling that
takes over feels worse than being bullied.

I examine the flabby ball and see what I
imagine
fear
dread,
two small holes, nostrils under

the nose Katy drew on Bouncy.

Holes a guy like Bouncy
doesn't need.

Can he be fixed? Katy asks.
Pig tape to the rescue, I say,
not telling her it's
Jill's fault
my fault
our fault that Bouncy needs first aid.

I feel a little better
knowing that the worst of a bad wish
can be fixed with pig tape.

If something is wrong with Dad,
all the pig tape, all the wishes,
won't help fix it.

PATCH

A patch of pig tape
in the shape of a heart gives
Bouncy a new nose.

We take turns blowing air,
watching the ball get round again.
A new nose for a faded
pampered
cared for
adored toy, one that would
not have holes to patch
if it weren't for the wish
probably.

Maybe there are some things
a wish can't fix,
a reminder that every wish
has a consequence.

As if I need
a reminder.

HOLES

I watch all day to see if anything else
has changed because of
the wish gone wrong.

Mom and Gran seem
the same. There are no holes
in anything else
as far as I can tell.

Pops comes home with
a surprise. Something to build,
a birdhouse kit in a box.
Hammer
nails
paint
will turn strips of wood into
a place a bird can call home.

I remember what Mom said about
keeping busy, keeping out
of trouble.
A birdhouse is the right thing
to keep me from
thinking about what is happening
at Jill's house.

Does everything seem the same there too?
Or did Jill find some holes?

Pops hangs the house
on a post, so we can see it when we look
out the kitchen window.

Darlene Beck Jacobson

It's fun building something again,
like Dad and I did
before he
got
lost.

GLUE

We started making airplanes when Katy was a
drooling
pooping
wailing
baby and Mom spent
most of her time taking care of her.

Dad set up a card table
in a corner of the living room,
our workshop for building airplanes.

Pieces so tiny, I was afraid of losing them or
messing things up until Dad said,
Small hands
are perfect for small planes.

No hammer or nails, just
a bit of glue holds it all together.
He laid out each piece,
showing me where to fit it.

A dab of glue from Dad.
A little drop is strong enough, Dad said.

I'd press on a wing or a door
while we talked about
Little League baseball,
Dad's first airplane ride, how he met Mom,
how much I was going to love my baby sister.

Building airplanes together,
just him and me, made me feel close to
Dad, like I could hold

Darlene Beck Jacobson

onto him, same as the wing held on,
thanks to the glue.

I guess the glue
holding me and Dad together
wasn't strong enough.

ROOM

On nights when it's too hot or it rains,
Katy and I sleep
in beds inside the house instead of
in the tent.

She shares a bed with Mom in
what Gran calls the
guest room, decorated with a
bedspread and curtains like they
have in a fancy motel.

The bed I sleep in is in the room
Dad had when he was a kid. Plaid
bedspread, dresser
with an oval mirror, and
a desk.

At first it was cool seeing all the
black and white pictures of Dad
dressed in his Boy Scout
and Little League uniforms.

All his school pictures from
kindergarten up to eighth grade,
in a frame with small rectangle
windows for each one.
A toothless kid with messy hair just like me.

I've been in this room
three weeks, four days, and a
million minutes, and now
it's weird seeing Dad
who isn't

108   *Darlene Beck Jacobson*

grown up, frozen in a kid world
without me
without Katy
without Mom.

Is the grown-up Dad in a room
somewhere wishing he was here?

If I don't know where Dad is or
what's wrong with him, how can I find
the right words
the exact words
the only words
that can bring Dad,
the whole, undamaged Dad that I remember,
home?

FLAG

After supper Pops watches the
evening news with Walter Cronkite.
Mostly I tune it out. Who wants to
listen to bad things happening
everywhere?

Tonight he tells about some soldiers
who have come home from
the war. I look up at the TV,
hoping to see Dad
or maybe other kids' dads,
hugging their families.

What I see instead are
coffins,
each one draped in a
flag, the US flag.

Just like when President Kennedy
died. His coffin was
in a parade
up and down the
streets of Washington, wrapped in a flag.
People saluting
staring
crying.

Dead soldiers coming home
is the worst thing you can see
on TV when your own Dad
might
could
maybe

Darlene Beck Jacobson

come home in a box wearing a flag.

The worst outcome for a wish to
bring him home.

I wish — far away from a listening fish —
I wish I knew
what to do.

NEST

It's only two days since we put up
the birdhouse and Gran said a
bird has moved in.

Katy wants to know what color bird,
and I want to know what kind.

We run outside, then
tiptoe to the box
so we don't scare the bird away.
Gran lifts the roof flap which is like
a door with hinges,
so you can see inside.

It's a nest of sticks,
grass, and feathers,
a perfect little bowl
holding three perfect little brown speckled eggs.

Where did the bird go? asks Katy.
Probably to find some food, Gran says.
It's not a robin, I say,
Because I've seen their blue eggs before.

Why don't you go to the library and
look up what kind of bird it might be?
Gran says as we follow her inside.

Darlene Beck Jacobson

BIRD

The library has a big book
with color photos and names
of all the birds that live around here.

The nice lady who
sits at the desk, the same one who gave me
the wishing stories,
is really interested in birds and
knows a lot about them.

She says our nest builder
is a common house sparrow,
nothing fancy or exotic, she says,
showing us a picture of
the mostly brown and white bird.

It's okay that it's plain, says Katy,
I like all birds.

I know what she means,
because just having a
bird
any bird
our own bird
in the house we made,
feels pretty neat.

KING

It's July fourth, fireworks at the park.
We wear red, white, and blue,
pack lemonade and popcorn,
squirt bug spray on our skin,
bring flashlights to find our way in the dark.

I hope I see Jill,
worry that I might see the rest of her family,
wonder what I will say if they're all
together pretending everything is okay.

Maybe they're not coming.

Then, behind us,
away from everyone else, I see them. Cody looking
but not looking at the man next to him.
Dale, sitting in a chair
instead of on a blanket like everyone else,
like maybe he thinks he's a king?

Jill's mom wears sunglasses,
a straw hat, even though it's
almost dark and there is no sun.
Jill looking everywhere for me?
I stand up, wave.

She gets up and is ready to run
until Dale says something to
Jill's mom who grabs
Jill's arm which makes her sit down again and
makes Cody look in my direction.

Cody waves, like we're best friends,

happy to see each other.

Who's that? asks Mom.
The giant pest, also known as
Jill's brother Cody, I say.

Seems like a nice, friendly boy
is what Mom thinks by the look on her face.

It's a mom's job
to see the best in everyone.

PULL

Things you pull:
rope in a tug of war
wagon which is easy
because of the wheels
teeth if they're loose
weeds if you're helping Gran in the garden
taffy because it's fun to see how far
you can stretch it
before it snaps.

When people say they're
pulling for you, it means
they hope things go well
turn out all right
or they're on your side.

Isn't it funny
how push and pull mean the
same thing
when you see a family coming apart?

Something or someone
pushes the family, pulls the family
and it tears
splits
comes apart like a piece of rotted cardboard.
Then you have to work
real hard to
push it, pull it back together.

All the
pig tape in the world
won't help.

Darlene Beck Jacobson

BOOM

Wowee booms are what Katy calls
fireworks since she learned
to talk. Wowee for what you see
bursting in the sky and boom for the
noise it makes a few seconds later.
It's the best definition
for something spectacular,
not like anything else.

Dad is the one
who likes to celebrate things
in a big wowee boom kind of way.

Even though these fireworks
are just as spectacular as ever,
there is something missing.

Someone who made
everything around us seem
louder
brighter
shinier.
I miss that kind of boom.

I imagine Dad staring at the
same moon, watching fireworks
like us, imagining that we are together.

Where are you, Dad? Are you MIA
in a place that has fireworks?
Can you see them,
hear them?
Are you someplace safe?

NOTE

Hi, Dad, did you see
wowee booms for the fourth of July?
I know it's about America's birthday and
there is no reason to celebrate
in a place far away, a Vietnam place in southeast Asia,
but you can imagine it, right?

Like when we watched from
the top of the skyscraper
that time we went to New York City.

Is your lost place like a city or like here?
When you close your eyes,
can you still hear it, hear us,
see us?

I wish I could talk to you about
some of the things going on here.
Would you believe in a fish
that makes wishes come true?

How do you get a kid to stop
bothering you? Should wishes be for
good things or bad things? Should wishes be
for yourself or someone else?

What would happen if I
wished you back? Would you come home
the same Dad or
would you have holes, like Bouncy?
Bigger
worse
unfixable holes.

Darlene Beck Jacobson

If you had
three wishes, what
would you wish for?
Love, Jack.

I tuck the note under my pillow. Maybe
it will help me have
a good dream,
not a nightmare, about Dad.

KNOW

Except for the fireworks, I haven't
seen Jill, mostly because
I'm afraid to leave the house, worried
everything might disappear
or change if I do. Or
I might disappear or change.

Hard to know how to act
how to be
what to do
about a fish that grants wishes.

Grownups don't believe in
fairy tales or magical things like
wishes coming true.

Jill knocks on the kitchen door.
Mom invites her in for
a slice of bakery cherry pie
and chocolate milk.

We eat with
Katy practically sitting in
Jill's lap, she's that close to her.

I know Jill has things to tell me.
Her knees bounce up and down as she sits
on the edge of the chair, instead of
tucking them under her like she usually does.

She looks at me,
the door, then
me again.

Darlene Beck Jacobson

We wolf down the last bite. I tell Mom,
We're going for a bike ride.

FAKE

Katy begs to come.
I want to ride on Jill's bike
with her, she
practically cries.

She's forgotten about Fred
and wishing, so she
needs to stay away from us
until we sort things out.

We're working on a surprise
for your birthday, I say.
Her birthday is next week, so
even though I
feel like a fake
phony
liar
Katy stops begging, and Jill
promises a ride tomorrow.

I can tell Katy is
excited, so I'd better
come up with something good
for her big day.

Katy will be five
which is still kind of little, but
she's smart enough
to know
a fake.

Darlene Beck Jacobson

STRANGE

I have to make my
last wish, is the first thing Jill says
when we
are away from other ears.

What happened when you
went home after the other wish? I ask.

Jill looks at me,
like I'm asking something strange.

Everything went back
to the way it was before, everyone
saw me
heard me
felt me. She shrugs.

I tell her about Bouncy and
holes. Something must be different,
maybe small, but we need to find out
before we make another wish.

Is Cody different? I ask, remembering
how
he waved to me at the park.
He still acts like a bully, Jill says.

Dale?
Same, says Jill.
Your mom?
Jill shakes her head, frowns.

One thing maybe, Jill says. Mom wears

sunglasses
all the time, inside and out,
even when it's dark. She only takes them off
to go to sleep.

Why? I ask.
Mom says looking at things without them
makes
her eyes hurt. She had her eyes checked.
Nothing is wrong.

It's a feeling, Mom says,
a feeling that something isn't right
when she looks at the world
without sunglasses.

Darlene Beck Jacobson

WARN

Do you think Fred is trying
to warn us about how wishes,
even good wishes,
can make things happen to people
who aren't part of the wish?

Jill is quiet, but I can
almost feel her thoughts as
we straddle our bikes.

Before she makes those
thoughts real, I say,
Maybe we shouldn't make
anymore wishes.

I just want Cody
to stop being a bully, she says
in a voice all choky, croaky
sad,
a voice that squeezes and chokes
my words and thoughts.

She blinks, rubs her eyes, looks at me.
What if I just wish that? For
Cody to stop being a bully. What could happen?
How would that hurt anyone?

He threw my sneakers
into the pond. I told Dale.
Dale asked Cody if he took them.
Cody told him I left them outside and
somebody else took them.

Dale said I need
to take better care of my things, not leave them
outside, even though
they were
under my bed.

Cody broke Mom's best vase
on purpose, blaming me
so Dale made me go to my
room without supper.

Mom didn't even listen when I
told her what happened. She just said,
Follow Dale's rules, honey,
and we'll all
get along.

Darlene Beck Jacobson

LIST

Riding around on our bikes,
me trying to figure out how to
make the mad fear in Jill's eyes
go away.

Jill just riding, not talking or
looking at me, like you do when you
have a fight with your friend
and it's too soon, too hard
to say you're sorry.

Making a list of the things
I imagine happening if Jill
uses her wish.

Cody stops being a bully.
Would Dale stop being a bully too?
Would Jill's mom stop
wearing sunglasses? Would she
see what's
really going on in her house?
Would I turn into
someone else, someone
I don't recognize?

What about Katy?
She wasn't part of Jill's wish, but it
rippled
rolled
touched her
and made Katy forget me.

I can't let that happen again,

can't watch Jill
riding like she's got nowhere to go, either.

Darlene Beck Jacobson

FEAR

Riding side by side, I
reach out and touch Jill's arm.
Stop, I say.

We skid onto the grass
under our favorite tree,
hide our bikes, climb, and
settle onto the branch.

No staring into each others' faces
this time,
but I can smell the fear in Jill's
sweat and
maybe in my own, too.

I swallow, wipe sweaty hands
on my T-shirt. It's your wish, I say,
and you can make it with
or without me saying okay.
I have to save my wishes, just in case.

In case? She looks up,
biting her lip,
frowning.

In case I figure out
how to bring Dad home
without making a mess of it, of him.

Are we still friends? Jill's sigh big enough
for both of us.

I nod my head, afraid that

if I open my mouth
to say yes, I'll cry.

WHEN

When are you going to
do it? I ask, wondering if it's
worse to wait or get it over with.

Even though you don't want me to
make the wish, Jack, I want
you to be there, to be sure I say it
right, don't mess it up.
Will you, Jack?

Okay, I say, When?

Now, before Cody and Brad
come back from the store.
Dale gave them a list of things
to buy, they have to get
everything
on the list, and then Cody gets back his bike.

If he gets his bike back, that means we'll
never be free of him chasing us.

Bring your net, Jill says, Because mine is —
Yours is still floating on the pond, I say.

THIRD

It's like Fred is waiting for us
because as soon as
Jill's worm touches the water,
she gets a tug.

I hold the net while she lowers Fred into it.
His mouth opens,
closes, like he's asking us,
What do you kids want now, you kids
who are never happy with
your wishes?

Jill takes a breath, then another.
I want, she says,
I mean I wish Cody would stop being a bully.

She looks at me, but I'm not
looking back because
maybe if I don't agree with her wish, if I
pretend I'm not part of it,
nothing will happen to me or my family.

That's the wish I want to
make, Fred, Jill says as
Fred's old fish eye winks,
blinks three times,
then disappears into the water.

Darlene Beck Jacobson

NEXT

We look at each other, me half expecting to
see Jill changed or something,
Jill like the last thing she wants to do
is leave me and go
back home.

What do you want to do next? Jill asks,
giving me the kind of look that
makes me think
she's worried I might not want
to hang out anymore.

Next week is Katy's birthday, I say,
And I promised her something special, so
help me think of what that could be.

Planning a birthday surprise seems
like a good way to keep moving, keep
doing what
I need to do to get through this summer
and the only way I know
to forget about wishing for awhile.

Five is a cool number, Jill says,
So how about making that
the special thing?
I can give her five bike rides, she says, smiling.

And I can give her five tickets
to trade in for anything she wants to do
for the rest of the summer, I say.
You can come to her party, right?

Wouldn't miss it, Jill smiles again, waiting
for me to smile back. I do,
but she knows it will be awhile
before I smile like I
mean it.

SICK

Will you come to my house so
we can see if things are, you know,
okay? Jill asks.

We ride side by side,
and the farther away from the water,
the pond, from Fred I get,
the more I feel like I
might puke. The feeling comes over me
when we start to ride away.

I gulp in air, hoping it will settle the
upsidedownness in my guts that
makes no sense.

Is this part of the wish? A
sour taste and a stomach
that refuses to be calm?
What does getting sick have to do
with anything?

You okay? Jill asks when
I don't answer her first question,
the one about going to her house.

I think I might be sick, I say.
All I can think of
is getting to Gran's house fast.
I'm going home, I tell Jill.

Do you want me to come with you?

Go to your own house.

Check for holes, okay?

Jill nods and
it isn't until she rides away that
my stomach feels normal again.

WHY

Is it my mind telling my stomach
to get upset because
I didn't do what I thought I should,
which was to stop Jill from
making the wish?

Or maybe my stomach got upset because
all I've been doing is
thinking about dumb wishes
holes
messed up stuff?

There has to be a
different answer besides
the one that keeps coming back to me,
the one about how
this last wish makes it impossible to be
around Jill without
feeling sick.

Dumb thoughts have to be
the reason. Like
the time I worried so much
about a test, I had to
go to the boys' room to puke
when it was over,
even though I got a B+.

Dumb thoughts make a stomach
and a boy
act dumb.
Time to think about other things.

BURP

A glass of cold
lemonade, chocolate pudding,
and a peach, taste like
the best food ever invented.

Makes me feel like I've
got my brain and guts back.

I let go with
a loud, frog-sounding,
what-a-relief burp that
makes everyone except Katy say, Jack!!!
in voices that mean
where are your manners,
you shouldn't burp like that
without saying excuse me!!!

Katy says, Teach me how to
frog-burp, Jack.

Even though everyone says
He
Will
Not
I wink and tell Katy
we'll give it a go before
lights-out in the tent.

Right now
I've got a special birthday to plan.

Darlene Beck Jacobson

FIVE

Mom, Gran, and Pops like the idea of
doing everything in fives for Katy's
big day.

We're having
five kinds of ice cream
five layers on the pink cake
five gifts to unwrap,
and I'm giving Katy
five tickets to play any games
or do anything she wants
without complaining.

Jill promised five bike rides and
even though her coming to the party
makes six people,
it wouldn't be the same without her.

Me and Mom are making newspaper hats
we're decorating with crepe paper
feathers
buttons
from Gran's sewing tin.

Katy is so excited, she's been spinning
in circles and singing the Happy Birthday song
to herself, reminding me of how
Dad could burp the tune without even trying.

It feels good making my little sister
happy, doing something,
anything, that has nothing to do
with wishing.

CALM

I don't want to lose the good feelings I
have from
planning Katy's party, so I decide
not to look for any holes
anywhere around me
until after the party.

Like Pops always says,
Leave well enough alone, which means
the same as
when Gran says, Let sleeping dogs lie,
which also means what
Mom tells me every time I get worked up
about stuff,
No need to make a
mountain out of a mole hill.

Funny how so many
of the sayings grown-ups use
all mean the same thing.

Stay calm
and cool and
all will be well.
Right now I'm Captain Calm,
mostly.

Darlene Beck Jacobson

DIME

Pops wants me to go
to the store with him so we can
pick out some toys for Katy's birthday.

We ride Pops' truck into town to the
store Pops calls the Five and Dime.
I wonder why it isn't called
Five and Ten or
Nickel and Dime, but the sign outside
just says F W Woolworth and Co.

Inside is a place where
wishes come true without a fish,
everything a kid could imagine.

We spend
forever
no time at all
not long enough
looking at every toy a kid could want.

But I remember we are here to pick
for Katy five things
a soon-to-be-five-year-old girl would want.
So after trying out a lot of things,
Pops and I find our favorites.

PICK

Pops is like
Santa Claus, wanting to pick out stuff
for everyone.

Not everyday we get to celebrate one of our
grandkids' birthdays, he says.

Here's what we pick for Katy:
A book by Dr. Seuss since Katy thinks
his books are funny.
A pink hula hoop. Actually, we get three,
a blue one for me and a red one for Jill.
Watercolor paints and paper.
A doll that cries
pees
looks pathetic
when you feed it a bottle of water.

It even comes with a diaper, though
why anyone would think
changing a diaper is fun
is a mystery to me.
I helped Mom do it once
when Katy was a baby and no way
would I ever do it again.

The biggest gift, the best one, is
a little-girl-size bike with training wheels.
Katy will flip out when she sees it for sure.

A bag of coconut-covered
marshmallows for Gran, her favorite,
and a bag of Tootsie Rolls for Mom.

Darlene Beck Jacobson

CALL

The day before the party, the telephone rings.
When I pick up and say hello,
Jill says hello back before she tells me
the worst news.

News that messes up birthday plans for Katy.

Both of us have to be at the party, she says.
You and me both are already coming, I say.

No, she says, both me and Cody.
I can't come unless Cody comes too, Dale said.

Why does Dale get to decide?
Who is he to mess up Katy's birthday?
I say it so loud,
I imagine Jill
jumps
stares
pulls the phone
away from her ear.

So I guess
I won't be coming, Jill says
in a squeaky, whispery voice that
really means she hopes it will be okay
to bring
him, her brother Cody.

We only have enough for six, I say, not seven,
which sounds mean when I say it, but is
less mean than what I'm thinking,
which is:

How can you mess up my sister's party
by bringing the town bully?

He always behaves when
there are grown-ups around,
Jill says, like she's reading my mind, hoping
this fact that sounds fake will
change it.

Knowing Katy will be sad if
Jill doesn't come to her birthday party
is what makes me finally say okay,
even though it is anything but
okay.

TELL

When I tell Mom that Jill has
to bring her brother
to the party, I remind her how
the whole five thing will be messed up
with seven people.

She pats my head. It was
messed up with Jill being six, but
that should not
be part of the count.

Any brother of Jill's is welcome here, Jack,
the more the merrier.
I'm sure we'll have a lovely time.

Lovely
is not the word I'd pick
to describe it.

IDEA

I didn't think Katy
could get more excited than
she usually is, but
the idea of Jill's brother,
someone she doesn't even know and
if she did she'd run away from him and hide,
the idea of Cody coming to the
party has Katy
buzzing
tingling
vibrating.

She wants name tags on the table to show
everyone where they sit.
Jill on one side of her, Cody on the other.

That's my seat, I say
trying to keep the mad out of my voice.

Silly Jack, you're my brother everyday.
My idea is for Jill and Cody to be my
pretend sister and brother for a day.

Standing with hands on hips
she means what she says, and
I don't have the
guts
nerve
heart
to tell her it's a rotten idea.

146   *Darlene Beck Jacobson*

WANT

I want
the day to be over and
it hasn't even started. I want
my stomach to stop making me feel sick.

I want
to stop worrying about Katy having
a rotten party
because of Cody. I want Mom
to stop being so nice all the time. I want
Gran to stop humming
the Happy Birthday song.

I want
Pops to take me away from here
just for the day. I want
to be brave enough
strong enough
smart enough to
stand up to Cody if I need to.

I want
Katy to be as excited
when it's just me
she gets to spend time with.

I want to call Dad,
talk to Dad. I want
Dad to come home,
to make all these wants
go away.

DOOR

Ding dong is the sound the
doorbell here makes
when you press it. At home
the doorbell buzzes like an
angry bee, sort of how
I feel right now. Makes me wish
I had a stinger.

Everyone is busy
with last minute getting-ready stuff,
so I am the one who has to answer the door.
It will be no surprise who
is on the other side.

I stand, hand on the doorknob,
thinking this would be something
maybe worth wishing about.

That makes me remember
the wish Jill made. Will
the boy who walks through this door
be a new and improved Cody?

Ding dong again.
I grit teeth, blow a puff of hot, mad air,
turn the doorknob, and open the door.

Darlene Beck Jacobson

WHAT?

Hi, Jack.
They say it at the same time,
wearing matching blue T-shirts and red shorts,
chewing gum and looking at me,
reminding me of the
Double Mint Gum twins from that TV commercial.

Except
Jill is wearing the kind of smile that you
put on when
you want someone to think you're happy,
but you really aren't.

Cody stares, eyes wide,
looking like an animal when it sees
the headlights from your car
and it freezes and can't move.

Thanks for inviting me, he says,
mouth twitching like he wants to smile but
doesn't know how.

A chill goes up and down my spine.
What is going on? I want to
scream
shout
shake him, but
everyone is standing behind me saying,
Come in and let's get the party started.

It's so nice to finally meet you, Cody, Mom says.
We've heard so much about you.

THIS

Katy gives Cody the full brother treatment,
asking questions about
anything
everything
nothing
as Cody stands and listens,
answering and barely moving, like
he's glued to the rug.

Of all the things
I imagined might happen
after the wish,
this is not one of them.

Is he playing a game,
pretending to be this quiet someone else,
so I let my guard down?
Trying to fool me into thinking
he can be trusted?

This version of Cody, this robot Cody,
is as fake as the snow in a can
you spray on a tree.

I have something to tell you, Jill says
as we slip into the living room
to be by ourselves.

LIED

You're going to be mad at me,
probably, Jill says.
But I had to do it or you wouldn't
believe me.

Do what? I ask.

She looks embarrassed
ashamed
determined
all at once as she says,
Dale didn't make me bring Cody.
I wanted him to come,
so you could see what happened
after the wish.

You lied? I thought we were friends
and friends
don't lie to each other. You
don't care if the party is
messed up because you want
me to
watch him, like a monkey
in the zoo?
This is Katy's day.
You had no right.

Jill wipes her eyes. I know, she says.
I'm sorry I lied, but
look at him! Ever since the wish, he
walks around like he's lost.

He follows me everywhere,

can't make up his mind
about anything, and
hardly speaks.

He wore the same clothes as me,
like he forgot who
he is
or was
or should be.
He's not a bully anymore, but
he's not anybody else either.

Jill grabs my arm, won't let me leave.
You told me
to look for holes, she whispers.

This one is so big and deep,
I don't know how to fix it.

I lied because I need
your help.

Darlene Beck Jacobson

SEE

Part of me
doesn't care that Cody is
quiet
confused
acting like a robot.

Isn't this one of those times to let
sleeping dogs lie, not stir up the pot?

But as I watch him playing
Pin the Tail on the Donkey,
watch how Katy tends to him,
like she does Bouncy,
I start to see what Jill sees.

A boy pretending,
wearing a costume that doesn't fit,
a boy who doesn't act like a boy at all.

When Katy shows Cody Bouncy,
tells him how the ball got the holes,
Cody breaks down
falls apart
bursts into tears,
like it's the saddest thing he's ever seen.

How can I not care?
What would you do, Dad?
Where are you when I need you?

ONCE

Dad cried once that I can remember, when I
was five years old like Katy.

We were at a park with a huge playground.
I was curious about the part
where the older kids played.

Dad promised to take me
to the spot after we ate.
I couldn't wait for what seemed like
forever. I wandered away when
Mom and Dad were talking to some friends.

The monkey bars were so high,
a big, round steel cage that looked like a
mountain to me.

It was easy to climb
all the way to the top.
I remember feeling like a tiger,
brave
fierce
powerful.

When I got to the top and looked down to
where I'd been, I froze, afraid to move,
to call out, to let anyone see me stuck there.

I started to shake.

The longer I squatted at the top alone, the more
I shook until my feet slid out from under me.

Darlene Beck Jacobson

When I woke up, Mom and Dad were crying.
Dad had me in his arms. You okay, Champ?
What happened? I asked.

You fell, hit your head, passed out.
Dad wiped his face on his shirt.
I thought, I was afraid we'd lost you, he said.

I'm right here, Dad, I said.

Don't ever wander off again, you hear me?

It was the only time
that Dad ever
raised his voice.

CAKE

A five-layer cake with pink frosting and
five candles sits in front of Katy
while she closes her eyes and makes a wish.

A quiet, silent one that Fred will never hear.

Katy huffs
puffs
blows
as we all cheer and the flames go out.

As pieces of cake get passed around,
I remember Katy's first birthday,
how all of us,
Gran
Pops
Mom
Dad
me
blew out pretend candles, laughing, trying
to get a
one-year-old to blow air,
to blow out her own candle.

She stared at us, like we were the
best entertainment, then
she grabbed a chunk of cake in her chubby fist,
smushing it into her mouth,
laughing.

I think that was when
I knew I'd love my sister
forever.

Darlene Beck Jacobson

KIND

What kind of ice cream do you like, Cody? asks Gran
when we're sitting around the table.

Everyone has a scoop of
chocolate
vanilla
strawberry
butter pecan
or orange sherbet.

Cody looks at Jill with her scoop
of strawberry and says, The same
as Jill, I guess.
You hate strawberry ice cream, Cody, Jill says.
You hate anything with strawberries, remember?

Cody sighs, frowns,
shakes his head. Then I don't know what kind, he says.

Jill looks like she might cry
until Katy smiles, pats Cody's arm.
Taste all of them until you find
the one you like, she says.

The rest of the day is just like that, Katy doing
one kind thing after another for Cody,
Mom, Gran, Pops beaming smiles,
me and Jill staring in disbelief.

It isn't hard to believe Katy is kind. She's
the princess of kind everyday.

What is hard to believe is

how a wish
that was supposed to help Cody
be a boy full of spirit,
a boy once kind himself,
turned him instead
into someone empty.

Darlene Beck Jacobson

KITE

The flat gift that Cody gives Katy
is a kite. Not a cheap-o one like you get at
the Sweet Shop for a dollar.
This one is silk, shaped like a butterfly
in orange, black, and yellow.

Like all the other gifts she opens,
Katy hugs the kite, calling it
the most beautiful one ever.

After she thanks Cody, she looks at him,
eyes wide, and says,
I had a dream about you,
a different you,
because I didn't really know who you were.

In the dream you were mean, so it
couldn't have been you. That
dream boy would never do
something so wonderful.

Cody looks at her for a
long minute, frowning like
he's trying to remember.

Does he remember the
in-between time of the wishes?

Will you help me fly the kite, Cody?
Katy waits for him to answer,
but all he can do is
nod his head, as if talking
is too much to bear.

GIVE

When the party is over and it's
time for Jill and Cody
to leave, Katy wants to give her hula hoop
to Cody. No, I say,
Cody can have the blue one.

Then you won't have one, Jack. Katy frowns.
It's okay, I say, handing the hoop
to a surprised Cody.

Cody stares at the hoop,
a small smile settling on his face.
Are we friends? Cody asks, looking at me,
the kind of look that is
hopeful
confused
wondering.

Jill stands behind him,
wide-eyed, nodding her head up and down,
looking just as hopeful,
confused, and wondering as her brother.

I give them the answer
the hard answer
the only answer
that makes sense to me.
I don't know if we're friends.

Let's meet at the pond tomorrow
after lunch, I say.
We have a lot of things to sort out,
to figure out what happens next.

Darlene Beck Jacobson

RISK

It's hard for me to fall asleep,
thinking of everything that has
happened the past few days.

Cody could be faking things, maybe, but
he sure seems to be a lost boy
who needs help.
My help
Jill's help
and maybe even Katy's help too.

I'm going to have to
take a risk
a big risk
the biggest risk
and talk to Cody,
tell him about the wishes and let him decide
what to do next,
because I think I figured out
what went wrong,
and we have to make it right.

At least we have to try.

NEWS

A knock on the door right after lunch
when I'm supposed to meet Jill and Cody
at the pond
could mean anything, since no one
has ever knocked all the time we've been here.

Mom just got back from the bakery, and
Pops and Katy are helping Gran
move the furniture
around the living room.

Katy's idea of help is riding around on the
sofa and chairs while Pops pushes them
to their new spots.

Answer the door, Jack, Mom says.

A man wearing a uniform with the words
Western Union on the shirt and hat
holds out a letter in a yellow envelope.

Is this the Jenkins household? he asks,
handing it to me when I nod.
He smiles, says, Have a good day.

Who was it? Mom asks, Did you…

When I hand her the envelope
the rest of her words get stuck as she
slumps into the chair,
a hand over her
mouth.

Darlene Beck Jacobson

PART

How come in school
they only teach you part
of what you need to know about things?

Knowing that Samuel Morse
invented a code and a way to
send messages
far away, faster than mail
is the part we learned in fourth grade.

They left out the part about
how when people get
telegrams, they are
so scared
so afraid
terrified
to open them.

How mostly a telegram isn't
good news, only bad.
The worst bad news would be
about Dad.

Gran
Pops
Mom
stare at the telegram on the table,
like it might be a scorpion or
poisonous snake.

It isn't until I say, Maybe it's from Dad
that Mom picks up the telegram and
opens it.

TELEGRAM

MR. MRS. JENKINS
YOUR SON CAPTAIN TODD JENKINS IS A
POW IN VIETNAM. CAPTURED ON APRIL 2.
HEALTH STATUS UNKNOWN.
WE WILL UPDATE YOU WHEN ANY NEW
INFORMATION IS OBTAINED.

WAR DEPARTMENT US ARMY

HOLD

Mom puts down the telegram with a shaky hand,
lets out a big breath of air, reaches out
her arms, and says,
Let's hold hands.

All of us,
even Gran and Pops, stand around the table
in a circle, holding hands, staring at
the yellow paper
the thing
the telegram
that tells us Dad is no longer lost,
no more MIA, POW instead.

Prisoner Of War.

Is Daddy coming home? Katy asks.

Eyes squeezed shut, still holding hands, Mom
shakes her head.

How is POW better than MIA? I ask.

He's been found. He's alive, Mom says,
And that is something we can
hold onto.

JAIL

All I can think about is
Dad being locked up like
prisoners are when
they are in jail.

He didn't commit a crime,
so is the prison he's in an okay place to be?

I guess my face must look awful
because Pops says, Don't worry Jack.
Officers are given
privileges other soldiers aren't.

He says this with a funny look on his face,
like maybe he wants to believe it
as much as I do.

Even if I lived in a fancy hotel room
with maid service and good food,
if the door was locked and
I couldn't
get out
go anywhere
be free,
it would stink.

Like a mind reader, Pops says
Todd can do it. He'll make it,
one day at a time.

He crushes me in a hug.
Stay strong and keep holding
onto hope. It keeps you going.

Darlene Beck Jacobson

JUNK

Part of me wants Katy to stay home,
away from the pond and Cody
and all the things we
have to talk about. She's too little.

She's also smart and doesn't have
a lot of junk stuffed in her head,
junk that tells you
how to act
who to be nice to
what's important.

Maybe we need somebody who can
ask the questions
we're afraid to and who sees good
in everybody and everything.

Get your bike, I say.
Where are we going, Jack?
On an important mission
to meet Jill and Cody at the pond.

Why is it important?
Remember when you met Cody yesterday,
how sad he was?
I cheered him up, Katy says.
You did, and you might have to do it again.

We have to find the real Cody,
the Cody who got lost when
Jill and I made a wish.

So the Cody who came to my party

was pretending? Katy frowns.

I don't know, but we might need
your help to find out. Okay?

Katy's legs pump harder as we ride the road
to the pond.

BREATHE

We find Jill and Cody lying on the grass
side by side, heads touching,
wearing the same matching outfits
from the party,
which makes me wonder,
did they even go home yesterday?

We park our bikes next to theirs. Katy skips,
plops down next to Jill, me next to Cody.

Hey, Jack, he says almost smiling.
We're watching all the things that fly around,
the things you don't notice when you're
standing up, he says.

We stay that way for a minute,
Jill naming the insects that buzz around
our heads, saying the
scientific names
while Katy squeals and gives each one
a name of her own.
Billy bee
Donna dragonfly
Abby ant.

The grass tickling my ear and the warm sun
on my arms and legs
makes me want to stay like this,
let things be as they are,
all of us just breathing and lazing,
no worries or thoughts to interrupt us.

The way summer

is supposed to be.

Katy jumps up, trying to capture a butterfly,
breaking the spell.

What are we going to
do? Jill asks as we sit up and brush grass
off our heads.

I look at Cody. Tell me about Dale and
how things changed when he came into
your life.

Darlene Beck Jacobson

OPEN

Know how when you
open the faucet on a hose without the
sprayer thingy, water gushes everywhere?
Cody talking is like the hose full blast.

Staring across the pond, his words spill out.
I was mad at Dad for leaving,
mad at Mom for giving up, for thinking
we were broken,
that we couldn't be a family anymore,
like there had to be another dad. When Dale
came around,
Mom was happy, happier than when
it was just us three.
Like Jill and me weren't enough.

That made me mad too. But Dale made Mom happy, so
I opened the door inside me and
let him in. Let Dale be
the dad Mom wanted us to have.

I did everything he asked to please him and Mom,
to keep the peace. Dale's talks about
being on top
being the best
being a winner, took away some of the mad.

When Dale stopped being nice, Mom
had already put her faith in him.

I told her about the things he'd say and do,
games and contests impossible to
win, punishments for losing.

She didn't hear
didn't listen
wouldn't see.

If I couldn't beat Dale, I'd join him. Then
maybe Mom would pay attention.

Darlene Beck Jacobson

BULLY

When Cody stops talking, Jill says,
That's when you stopped being the
brother I knew and turned into
someone else.

Cody breathes a sigh so heavy,
Katy takes his hand, squeezes, and says,
You made a mistake but that's okay,
because we're going to help you. Right, Jack?

I nod, so glad
I decided to bring her along.

Cody looks at Katy, then Jill, says,
I liked the feeling of being in charge,
showing Dale and Mom I didn't need them,
didn't need anybody. No one
paid attention when
I was nice. Mom didn't care.

I did, Jill says. Did you forget we used to
be a team like
Jack and Katy, doing everything together?

Cody squeezes back tears. I got so good
at being mean, I didn't need a sister anymore.
Sorry, he whispers, head hanging.

Katy asks the important question.
Do you still want to be a bully?

When I did something mean, Cody says,
My heart beat faster and I felt alive.

Now I feel like I want to throw up
and my head hurts.
I don't know how to be anything else.

That's why we're here, Jill says.

What made you stop being
a bully, Cody? Katy asks.

Cody shrugs. Jill and I look
at each other.
We need to tell you both
about the wishes.

Darlene Beck Jacobson

SASS

Katy with eyes like a frog that never blink,
Cody frowning, forehead wrinkled like Gran's,
me and Jill taking turns telling about
Fred and the three wishes.

Cody shakes his head. A fish that
grants wishes is
crazy, he says. That can't be the reason,
no way, makes no sense.
He paces the grass, back and forth
along the pond, hands over his ears,
refusing to listen as we try to explain.

Katy stops Cody with a stare,
hands on hips, making him open his ears.
It's true, Katy says. I forgot
about Fred. He made
my pancakes-for-supper wish come true, and
Jack doesn't fib or lie anyway.

And if you don't believe him or me or Jill,
maybe you don't want to be
a nice boy.
Maybe you don't want to
be my friend.
With a little sass and a whole lot of
sense, Katy gets Cody to listen.

The hardest part of the story
comes next, I say as we
sit back down on the grass.

Katy sits so close to me, I feel her breathe.

HELP

We tried to help you,
stop you from doing mean things
when we made the wishes, Jill says.

But every time we made a wish, something
bad happened,
something we didn't expect, didn't
wish for, I say.

Nothing bad happened when
I wished for pancakes, Katy says.

I'll tell you what I think about that
after we talk about the
weird things, okay?
Katy nods and listens.

Jill explains wish number one,
being invisible.
Number two made Mom
wear sunglasses all the time, she says,
And gave Bouncy his holes, I say.

The third wish, the last wish,
brought you here. Has anything else
changed at your house? I ask Cody and Jill.

Mom still wears sunglasses.
What about Dale? I ask Cody.
Dale is the same. Cody frowns.
Except now he's mean to…

Jill sucks in air, finishing what Cody started.

Darlene Beck Jacobson

Now Dale is mean to Mom, yelling and
making her cry.

It's like the mean that left Cody
didn't disappear,
it went inside Dale, and now Mom…

Cody stomps a foot at Jill, says,
Mom is punished because of you!

It's your fault, Jill, your fault, Jack!
You and your dumb wishes
that sound more like tricks.
Why couldn't you leave me alone?

You've messed up everything and
we'll never be able to fix it.
Stay away from me,
all of you.

He hops onto his bike and
rides away.

DONE

What have we done is all I can think as
Cody disappears from sight.

He's right to be upset,
mad, fed up with us,
exactly how I feel about all that's happened
in this place I didn't want to be. But now
I want to make the most of this summer
before it's over.

It's summer, I say.
There are still things to do, fun things.
Katy's face tells me she's ready for fun.
Jill needs to be convinced.

He'll be back, I tell her, because a part
of me knows he will.
How can you be sure? Jill's doubt
makes her body limp, floppy, like a rag doll.

Cody needs time, like we did, to figure
things out, I say.
What if the mean part, the bully,
is still there? Jill asks.

I think about myself, people I know.
Everybody has a mean part, I say.

When I feel mean,
doing things I like with friends
makes the mean go away. Then I'm done
moping
worrying

Darlene Beck Jacobson

being scared.

Cody will find his way back. Until he does, we
make plans, shake things up,
have some fun. When he needs us,
we'll be here.

Jill straightens up, nods, blows out the sad air,
shouts,
Last one to the tent is a rotten egg!

Jill and I smile, wink, and let
Katy lead the way.

SUMMER

Making a list of all the things
we want to do
before summer is gone takes up
the afternoon.

Katy's list: swim in a pool,
have a dress-up parade riding our bikes,
roller skate,
eat banana splits at the Sweet Shop.

Jill wants to see a drive-in movie,
have a scavenger hunt,
learn to play badminton,
spend one whole day speaking Pig Latin.

Or-fay eel-ray? I snort at Katy.
Ill-jay is azy-cray, twirling my
fingers in circles next to my head.
Katy asks, What's ill-jay? I point
Ill-jay, Atey-kay, Ack-jay,
laughing as Katy chants our
Pig Latin names while spinning in circles.

What do you want to do, Jack? Jill asks.
More of this, I say as I
join Katy for a spin, laughter loosening
my chest, lifting my spirit.

Maybe keeping busy will help me decide
how to use the wishes for Dad. Sometimes when
you're not thinking about
something all the time,
an answer has room in

Darlene Beck Jacobson

your brain to
show up.

GAME

Gran takes a break from gardening vegetables,
canning and food stuff,
joining me and Katy on the big oval
living room rug
for a game of Candy Land. It's our
third go 'round, the first one with Gran.

Laughing and being silly is
what made Gran stop her chores
take off her apron
plop down on the rug.

Having Gran to ourselves,
because Mom and Pops
are working, feels special.
Our reward for choosing to enjoy a
summer day.

Gran's cheeks as pink as Katy's,
eyes sparkling like
when you discover something
new, something you didn't realize
you missed until you have it.

Finding out that Gran cheats,
not so she wins the game, but so Katy wins.
The squeal of excitement,
Katy not noticing Gran's card shuffling,
is all the reward both of us need.

That was fun, Gran says,
But now I have some gardening to do.
Why do you grow

Darlene Beck Jacobson

so many vegetables anyway? I ask. Since it's
so much easier
to buy them at the store.

When you grow food, you never
have to worry about being hungry. Gran smiles
and gives us each a peach and kisses
on our foreheads.
Her breath smells like the
spearmint she grows in the garden.

Gran turns on the
radio that
sits on a shelf in the kitchen.
It's like the one I have
back home
that I forgot to bring.

I expect to hear
oldie
moldy songs like
the ones Pops always plays
on his radio in the truck.

Instead
"I Want To Hold Your Hand"
comes out of the tiny speaker.

It's impossible
not to smile when
I hear Gran sing along.

I didn't know you like the Beatles, Gran, I say.
Gran winks at me and
picks up her garden basket.

SEED

Gran? I ask before she heads outside.
Do you believe in miracles
or wishes coming true?

Gran smiles and says,
Every time something I've planted
in the garden
pops up through the soil,
it's a miracle.

That something wonderful
can start with a tiny seed,
be nurtured and grow,
is the best kind of miracle.

The way she looks at me
and Katy,
I know she's talking about
more than vegetables.

Darlene Beck Jacobson

SOBS

Remember those wind-up toys that
spin
race
dance in a circle
when you turn the key? They were
fun for awhile, until
you turned the key
one time too many, wound it
too tight. Then it got stuck with
nowhere to go.

I think that's what happened to Mom.

Last night when I snuck
into the kitchen for a midnight snack, I heard
crying
coming from the room Katy
shares with Mom.

I stopped outside the door
to listen, thinking
it might be Katy having a bad dream.

Then I heard the
honk-honk,
the breaking-the-sound-barrier
nose-blowing noise
Mom is famous for.

I tapped on her door. You okay, Mom?

It's a long minute before the door opens.
Mom peeks out, eyes and nose

the color of strawberries.

What's wrong, Mom?
I'm okay, she says,
sniffing and wiping her eyes. I
needed a good cry and I got one.

What's a good cry? I ask because
all the times I remember crying were
anything but good.

All the things we've been holding onto,
I've been holding onto,
needed a little release, she says,
as a shiver makes her
body twitch.

Like a broken wind up toy, I want
to say, because now I know
what she means.

How many other nights, nights
when Katy and I slept in the tent, how
many of those nights did
Mom have a good cry?
Alone.

Wearing her all-is-well mask every day,
holding onto hope and
everything else about as tightly as
a Band-aid holds up a wall. Which is
barely
hardly
really not at all until
she is alone and the mask disappears.
I think we both need some ice cream, I say.

Darlene Beck Jacobson

As we head to the kitchen, Mom says,
You're a good boy, Jack. Dad
would be
so proud.

We plow our way through a quart of
vanilla fudge, holding hands
across the table, listening to
our spoons clacking
the clock ticking
wind whistling through
the open window
above the sink.

DESK

I go back to Dad's room,
the room I sleep in, still too
wide awake
to get back into bed.

All the weeks I've been here,
I've never sat at the desk. It
felt too much like school.

I do it now, sliding
slipping
settling into the soft leather chair,
the same chair Dad sat in.

Opening drawers,
expecting to find something
anything
one thing of Dad's.

One drawer is full of Boy's Life magazines.
I'll read them later.
Another drawer holds a ruler, paper clip,
stapler, other desk things.

The top drawer, the smallest one,
has only one thing in it. A
key taped to the bottom.

I peel off the tape, finger
the key, trying it on the desk drawer
and the room door. No luck.
I go to sleep wondering,
where is the lock it opens?

Darlene Beck Jacobson

LAZY

Our usual Saturday morning
TV blitz, the one day we have the
TV to ourselves, is the
best kind of lazy.

Two bowls of Sugar Pops,
two cartoon shows picked by Katy,
Quick Draw McGraw and
Mighty Mouse Playhouse. My two picks
are the Adventures
of Rin Tin Tin about a hero dog
and Roy Rogers, a hero cowboy.

Even in a cartoon TV world, kids
are having adventures, on
a quest,
braving the unknown.

Part of me likes the
lazy Saturday feeling, body
glued to the floor, eyes
glued to the black and white world,
a lazy
hazy
crazy way to spend a morning.

But this Saturday, a
bigger part of me is ready for
a quest of my own.

A quest to find the lock
that can be opened
with Dad's key.

DUST

Everything that used to be
in Todd's room is in
the attic, Pops says when I
show him the key.

He had a box he kept
favorite things in. That's
probably what the key opens.

Up the creaking
squeaking
wobbly stairs
into the attic is a
time travel trip to another
universe, a universe covered
in dust.

A baby crib, carriage, high chair,
board games, trunk of old clothes,
lamps, and discarded furniture,
decorated in dust.

Stuffed in a corner, a three-legged chair.
Why does Pops save it
if it only has three legs?
Under the
chair is a box. A bulging
rectangle, taped closed,
marked TODD'S THINGS.

I pick up the box, blow off the dust,
sending a cloud to settle
somewhere else.

Darlene Beck Jacobson

It feels solid
and full in my arms, my
anticipation growing
with
each
step
down
the
stairs.

LOCK

Pops says, It's okay to
open the box. He, Gran,
Katy, and Mom stand around the table
like we've just dug up
a buried treasure.

My hands shake as I slice open
the tape holding down the flaps,
lifting them to peer inside.

Trophies, banners, report cards,
yearbook, a crumpled sweater
with a giant red letter sewn on it. A
letter Dad got for baseball.

Under all of it, sits a metal box.

I slip the key from my shorts pocket,
slide it into the lock,
and turn.

The lock pops open.

Darlene Beck Jacobson

BOOK

It's a book, I say,
trying not to show the
disappointment I feel. Don't know
what I expected. Something
exciting
thrilling
adventurous.
Something other than a book.

Todd wrote his thoughts and
feelings in that book, Gran says. When he was
going through a rough patch.

Personal, journal-like things? Mom asks,
meaning we shouldn't look at it.

I think your dad would want
you to read it, Pops says.
In a quiet place, when
you're alone, Gran says.

I look at Mom. Do you want
to read it first? I hope she'll
say no.

Reading my mind, she says,
You go first, sweetheart. One
boy to another.

I hug the black leather book
to my chest, almost feeling a
heartbeat
a breath

a hug from Dad in return.

When I open the first page,
I gasp
fumble
nearly drop the book.

Written in Dad's familiar
half-printing half-writing scrawl
are the words,
Wishes, Dares, and
How to Stand Up to a Bully.

Gran's right. This is a book I need
to read alone,
out of sight
later tonight
in my room.

Just me and Dad.

Darlene Beck Jacobson

TRIO

With Dad's book
safely tucked away until
tonight, we begin
our quest
to do everything on our
summer list. With less than
three weeks of summer left,
we have no time to waste.

The three of us,
a trio of adventurers, like the
Three Musketeers, except sometimes
we act more like the Three Stooges,
goofing around
to see who can be the silliest.

Mostly
Jill wins that contest, making Katy
think having her around
all the time is her best dream come true.

How's Cody? I ask, because
even though I'm
having fun doing this summer
adventure thing, I can't
help myself or
stop myself
from thinking about him.

Next to Dad's, his face pokes into my
brain, both of them
pushing for attention.
I have to do something,

use the power of the wish soon,
before we leave this summer place.

Maybe Dad's book has the answers
to all the questions I've been
carrying around in my head.

The biggest question, how could
Dad, when he was a kid like me,
write about things like
wishes
dares
and bullies?

How did he know it
might be important?

Jill interrupts my thoughts,
answering the question I asked her.

Cody stays in his room all the time,
only comes out to eat,
use the bathroom, Jill says.

That's sad, I say.

But Mom took off her
sunglasses while we ate supper,
staring at Cody most of the time. When we
finished eating and Dale left the room,
she asked me, Do you think something
is bothering Cody?

Yes, I told her.

Then let's have

a family meeting to talk about it, she said.

Without Dale? I whispered to Mom.
Without Dale, Mom agreed.

SING

Mom came up with a list for our
scavenger hunt, so we set out
with a canteen of water and peanut butter cookies.

Five different kinds of leaves
Five different colored stones
Feather
Pinecone
Empty bird nest
A stick shaped like a letter of the alphabet
A piece of string
A candy bar wrapper

After reading over the list, we
decide the best place to find most of the items
is the school playground which Jill says is
next to a park.

To kill two birds with one stone as Gran says, which
doesn't mean we're going to hurt any birds,
but really means
doing two things at once,
we decorate our bikes and dress like pirates, with
bandannas and eye patches, Katy wanting to pretend
we're looking for pirate treasure,
like we did at the lake.

Riding like we're in a parade on our way
to the hunt, listening to Katy sing
"The Song That Never Ends"
in the squeaky voice of Lamb Chop, the puppet
from the Shari Lewis TV show.

Darlene Beck Jacobson

Singing it
over and over
again,
giggling every time Jill and I
groan.

HUNT

After finding most
of the stuff on our list, we stop the hunt
for a snack break, sitting
on a bench
under a tree
in the park.

Grown-ups walking by
give us strange looks when we yell
pirate words.
Taking turns sipping from the canteen,
water dribbling down our chins because
we are laughing so hard, we
make ourselves gag.

Calling each other by our
Pig Latin pirate names, telling
knock-knock jokes, and having
just the kind of day I imagined.

A hanging-out-with-Dad
kind of day.

A day too good to last.

Darlene Beck Jacobson

WOLF

We ride over to the
schoolyard, park our bikes in the slots
of a rack
made just for bike parking.

A trio of two wheelers shining,
like mama, papa, and baby bikes
waiting for the three bears.

In this story, Goldilocks
arrives
dressed up like Brad, who's really the
big
bad wolf
ready to
huff
puff
blow away all the
good feelings we three little pigs
brought with us.

He spots us, heads in our direction, smiling?
More like sneering,
out to conquer the world or this
small part of it.

Looks like trouble found us, mateys, I say
as I stand up to face the
Wolf.

BRAD

Pretty early for Halloween, you losers
is the greeting we get, a greeting
none of us return.

What's with your brother? Brad asks Jill.
He got the plague or something? He
won't even come out of the house? Acts like a
sissy, just like the rest of you.

Brad spits, a slimy
green glob that looks like a slug
landing on my sneaker. A spit dare, a
what-are-you-going-to-do-about-it
spit. One that makes
Jill and Katy jump up, ready to fight
all for one
one for all,
hands on hips.

Pig Latin, go! I say,
and Jill and I launch into a
tirade of speed-talking nonsense
accompanied by Katy's
"Song That Never Ends," all of it
aimed directly at Brad who,
unable to speak our languages of choice,
walks off into the sunset,
shaking his head.

I rub the top of my sneaker in the grass
until all the slimy spit disappears.

Who was that? asks Katy.

Darlene Beck Jacobson

Another bully, Jill says.

A friend of Cody's, I say, And it looks like
we — the three of us — made a bully stop
without the help
of a wish.

WEAK

What made you think of that, Jack?
That Pig Latin, make enough noise and
the bully gets tired
and bored
and goes away cure? asks Jill.

Been thinking a lot about Cody, Dale, and why
people choose to be mean, I say.
Bullies pick on those they think
are weak
scared
afraid to fight back.

We have the best weapon for
fighting back.
Friendship.
When we stick together,
look out for each other,
we're stronger
bigger
braver than when we're alone.

Just like a bully chooses to be mean,
we can choose to be brave.

Jill nods, holding one index finger
in the air. It will take
more than being brave to stop
a bully like Dale, she says.

No, I say, it will take all of us,
Cody and your mom included.
Bullies need our permission to

rule over us.

Starting today, I refuse to give them
my permission. I stand
hands-on-hips superhero Katy style.

What if you don't know how
to be brave? Katy asks.

You're the bravest
five-year-old I know, I tell her.

RUSH

A long exhausting day of
hunting
searching
chasing bullies
and now,
when I should be ready to slow down,
I rush through supper,
helping Mom with dishes, skipping
a bath and clean pajamas
in favor of a night alone.

Katy begs to sleep in the tent.
It's been five whole
days since we've been there, Jack, she says.

Tomorrow, I say. You need to be in
your own bed, I need to be in mine.

Katy stamps
pouts
puffs
her displeasure, whining all the way
to the bedroom.

My guilt lasts only
a minute as I rush to
the bathroom, brush teeth, listen to the
angry thumps of Katy's feet
up and down the hall
outside the bathroom door.

It's time for me and Dad.

Darlene Beck Jacobson

MISSING

I slither down
the hall, slip into
the room, slide into bed,
switching on the bedside lamp.

I reach under the pillow,
pull out nothing?

Groping
grabbing
gasping
I toss the pillow across
the room, rip off sheets,
lift up mattress,
upend the bed and
the room, everything now
a wreckage
disaster zone
rumpled heap of scattered debris,
the aftermath of
a storm of rage.

Where is the book? I
know I put it
under the pillow, can
picture myself doing it.

So where did it go?

A book doesn't
fly, walk,
disappear without help.

Who would take a special
book, the most
special book, knowing
it means
the world to me?

Darlene Beck Jacobson

CLUE

Three pairs of eyes stare at
me, wondering what's up.

I put Dad's notebook under
my pillow, I say. It's not
there, not anywhere in
my room.

My voice
face
attitude must be
accusing, daring, because
all three
Gran, Mom, Pops say,
We haven't seen it, but
we'll help you look.

Going through Todd – Dad's – box
again, opening drawers
closets
cabinets. Searching
in, on, under,
over, behind, around each
room of the house,
even in the bathtub. Dumping
the trash full of dinner scraps
on the kitchen floor, just to make
sure.

Only place left is
Mom's room where Katy
snores and dreams, eyes
fluttering behind closed lids.

We'll search here
tomorrow, Mom whispers. We'll
find it. Books don't walk away
by themselves, she says.

As I watch Katy's chest
move up and down, I
wonder. Maybe,
certainly
surely
a book can move
with the help of a
five-year-old.

Katy was mad enough
at me
to find her own
mean.

KEEP

Why did you take the
Dad book and not tell me, I ask
Katy when she comes to the
kitchen for breakfast.

Rosy cheeks turn pinker,
brown eyes flash. I
was mad and sad, so I
did something bad, she says.

You didn't want to
be with me in the tent. You
wanted to be with the
book daddy,
without me.

He's my daddy too.
I wanted to keep the book so
you would come back
to me.

Her liquid eyes,
quivering chin
dissolve
melt
unravel my fury. I
blow away an
angry cloud,
grab her in a hug.

I never left you, I say. I
promise, pinkie-swear
promise, I'll read

everything in the book
to you. But I have
to read it first. Alone, I whisper.

Why? Katy sniffs.

It's a book of wishes and
a plan.

Katy wipes her eyes. What
kind of plan?

Taking care of a bully plan, I say. Maybe
something more is
what I hope but don't say.

Katy's sigh of understanding
fills the room.

She runs out the kitchen door
into the tent, the only place I
didn't search. She hands me
the notebook, wrapped
like a baby
in one of her doll blankets.

I'm sorry, Jack, she whispers. I
didn't know Daddy
was going to help us.

I didn't either, I say. Thanks
for taking good care of the book.

When I hand her back the blanket, she
uses it to
wipe her eyes.

Darlene Beck Jacobson

BILL

Back in my room, I
open the book past the
page that says *Wishes, Dares, and
How to Stand Up to a Bully* to
the one that tells
the story of a boy named Bill.

September   Sixth grade

*Bill Belcher is one year older than me
and one grade ahead. Ever
since second grade, he latched
onto me, always seemed to show
up no matter where I was.*

*Acting friendly at first, I
thought he wanted us to be buddies.*

*In those early years, he
did small things, taking some
of my cookies, asking to see a toy and
then accidentally on purpose
breaking it. Daring me to do
something, laughing when I couldn't.*

*Not being mean exactly, but
making me feel sad, unsure,
uncomfortable.*

*Small things turned into big things after I
made a friend.*

ENVY

Kevin Fisher was a new boy in
my class in third grade. He liked
all the same things I did and we
never ran out of things
to talk about or things to do.

The friendlier we got, the more
Bill tried to pull us apart. Telling me lies
about Kevin and telling
Kevin lies about me, trying
to get us to fight each other.

Pulling us down with
words, making us doubt
each other and ourselves.

Bill
did everything he could to
cause trouble for me and Kevin.

Today, the first week of sixth
grade, Kevin said he
didn't want to hang out
anymore. It's too much trouble, he said.

Without Kevin, it's
going to be a lot harder to stand up
for myself and fight off Bill.

The next page in
the book
is Dad's list of
wishes and dares.

Darlene Beck Jacobson

Wishes

I wish I was brave.
I wish I was strong.
I wish I was daring.
I wish I knew how to make Bill stop.
I wish I could still be friends with Kevin.

Dares

I dare myself to:

Find out why Kevin really stopped
being my friend. Friendship is always
hard, that's not a good enough reason.

Tell Bill to pick on
someone his own size.

Find out why Bill wants to be a bully.
It is a choice, isn't it?

Then there is a
whole page where all
Dad writes is:

I am not writing anything else
in this book unless
until
something changes.

I close the book, not
because there's nothing else to read, but
because there is so much to
think about in what

I've just read.

Dad had to deal with a bully and
he made some wishes, like I did. Only
there is something
different
about his wishes, different from the
ones Jill made for Cody.

NAME

When I read what I
just read a second time, I
remembered something that made
me feel funny the
first time I read it.

Why does the name Bill Belcher
sound familiar? Is he related to
Mr. Belcher, the nice man
who owns the Sweet Shop?

Maybe I can go over there and
ask Mr. Belcher if
he knows anybody
named Bill.

Just when I decide that's
what I'll do
tomorrow, a different thought
pokes at me. This one sends a
shiver
quiver
ripple
over my body.

Could Mr. Belcher, the
man who always smiles when
Jill and I come into the store, could
he be the boy,
now a man
named Bill? A man who
looks around Dad's age and not
Pops' age.

Was he the bully who,
once upon a time,
tormented Dad?
I sigh away my impatience
for wanting an answer now.
Waiting one
more day
will have to be okay.

I plan on using the time for
thinking about Dad's wishes,
why they seem different from
the wishes Jill made.

DRIVE-IN

I don't have time to read or think or worry
because tonight Pops has a treat for us.
We're going to see a drive-in movie.

The drive-in is a parking lot filled with cars,
and at every space there's a post
with a speaker that you clip onto
the front window of the car
so you can hear what's happening on the
giant, enormous,
as-big-as-the-side-of-a-building screen.

Mom, Pops, and Gran in the front seat,
me, Katy, and Jill stuffed in the back
with blankets,
snacks and drinks,
watching Katy's
favorite movie called *Flipper*
about a really smart dolphin
who saves a boy named Sandy from killer sharks.

Katy flops around behind the backseat,
in the flat part of the station wagon, pretending to be
a dolphin, squeaking like Flipper does
when he talks to Sandy.

Even though Flipper is
a mammal like humans are, he
reminds me of Fred,
the two wishes I have left, and
how summer is slipping
away, like a fish in water.

When the wish, the pancake wish,
was used to give something
instead of taking away something, it worked
without holes.

That's what was different about
the wishes Dad wrote in his book!
When Dad wished to be brave and strong
he didn't want that because
he wanted to be a bully. He wanted
to be able to
stand up to
a bully and stand by
a friend who
gave up on him.

His wishes are about how
he behaves, not
how others do.

Asking for things that
give instead of take
are the right kind of
wishes.

Darlene Beck Jacobson

WAKE

On the way home from the
drive-in movie while Katy sleeps,
Jill whispers, I can't hang out tomorrow.
Why? I whisper back.

We're going to my
Nana's house because Mom wants to see her.
Dale wanted to go too, but for the first time
Mom told him no. She wanted to see
Nana without him.

He wasn't happy when
Mom took off her sunglasses and
looked at him for a long time,
like when you have a staring contest
to see who looks away first. Dale did and
left the room.

Mom needs to ask Nana an important question
face to face, and we,
Cody and me, need to be there with her.
She promised to talk with Cody and
listen to all the things that have happened.

Without Dale around maybe
Mom will wake up
from sleeping with her eyes open.
Cross your fingers for us, okay? Jill asks.

I cross them on both hands, then
we spend the rest of the ride thinking our
own thoughts. Mine being a question.

Is wishing
Dad home a giving wish
or a taking wish?

Darlene Beck Jacobson

PACK

Pops doesn't know anyone
with a pool, so he's ready to go
to Woolworth's to buy a kiddie one, a pool
so small that when you
step into it, you might,
maybe if you're lucky, get your knees wet.

How can I be a dolphin
in a bathtub pool? Katy asks.

Pops scratches his whiskered chin.
He always has whiskers on Saturday
because he doesn't shave.

I have an idea, he says. Pack
your swimsuits and an overnight bag.
Where are we going? I ask.
To a sleepover at a motel outside the city,
one with an outdoor pool
big enough for a dolphin and the rest of us.

Pops pats Katy on the top of her head.
She's already practicing dolphin talk,
clicking and squeaking her delight, as
we pile gear into
the station wagon for a road trip to
Howard Johnson's.

Will Jill have time for fun on her road trip?

I get up early and
go to the Sweet Shop first thing
in the morning, but Mr. Belcher isn't at the store.

He'll be back
tomorrow, the lady in charge says.

I'm bringing Dad's book on the road trip to
see what happens. Does Dad talk about
Mr. Belcher again?

Darlene Beck Jacobson

POOL

Wearing a blow-up dolphin swim ring we found
at a hardware store near the motel, Katy
is so excited she could probably float
without it.

We have the whole shallow end
of the pool to ourselves,
most folks on lounge chairs instead of swimming.
The water is just cold enough
to make you suck in air when
you first jump in, but
not so cold you want to get out.

Me and Mom swim back and forth
across the pool, pretending
to be sharks while
Flipper, known as Katy on land,
rescues Gran and Pops.
By the time we get out of the water,
my toes and fingers are as wrinkled as raisins.

We eat pizza,
drink orange fruit punch
in the motel room while Mom
clicks away on the Instamatic camera,
trying to freeze this special day,
a day to share with
Dad when he comes home,
our lives without him captured
in pictures.

Will the pictures show the real me?
The coward who could bring Dad back

with one perfectly-worded
wish.

A coward too afraid of what
might happen if he said the wrong wish.

Darlene Beck Jacobson

CAGE

Mom and I sneak down to
the motel lobby in our pajamas
while everyone sleeps, looking for
snacks from a
vending machine. Trying to decide
which candy bar I want and which one to get
for Katy for the ride home tomorrow.

A squawk comes from the counter,
making me wonder how a bird flew
into the room.
My ears follow the second squawk
to the bird making it,
a bird trapped in a cage.

It flaps its wings, going nowhere, pecking
at the door,
hoping the right number of taps will
be the secret code that opens it.

A bird in a cage is
like someone in jail.

No matter how much you
stretch your wings, squawk,
bang on the door,
you can't get out.

Are you in a cage, Dad? A
place with no room to
spread your wings? Do
people, kind people, answer
when you knock?

Do you feel better being a prisoner
than when you were MIA?

Do you have someone
a buddy
another POW person
helping you
being kind to you
until you can come home?

If I wish you back, will it break you
or are you already broken?

Here's your candy bar. Mom
hands me the Reese's Peanut Butter Cup.

I walk over to the cage,
break off a chunk of the candy, offer it
to the bird.
He tilts his head at me,
snaps up the treat, swallowing it whole.

How come every time I
feel ready
to make the wish and
bring Dad home, something
like a cage
a coffin
a nightmare
reminds me how
dangerous all this wishing
can be?

DARE

Mom and Katy asleep in
the other motel bed, Gran and Pops
snoring so loud, I hear it
through the wall next door.

Perfect time for another visit
with Dad.

June   Last Day of School

We went to the lake to
celebrate a summer away from school. Six
of us – me, Kevin, three guys from
our class who we started
palling around with – and Bill,
inserting himself in our group, bullying
his way in.

Kevin and I had only
just started
being friends again. I walked up to him after school one day
and said I missed doing things
together. Can we give it another try?
Kevin agreed and we went to the lake,
just like old times.

Today, I didn't care if Bill showed up.
I was glad it was summer.
Kevin and I had plans.

We were swimming,
doing silly dives,
back flips, cannonballs, who can make

the biggest splash. Everyone wet except
Bill, standing at the water's edge,
name calling and boasting,
hurling insults and dares.

It was Kevin who said, Shut up, Bill. I
dare you to jump into the water from the
branch of that old tree.

I'd climbed that tree, sat on the branch
close to the trunk. Never slid
to the end, the part that
hangs over the water.

We all stared at Bill. I
wouldn't take the dare, even if it
meant being called chicken.

He didn't look like he wanted to, either.
But he'd spent
years trying
to convince us of
his courage
his bravery
his daring. Daring we'd
only heard about, never
actually seen.

With his reputation on the line,
Bill climbed the tree,
sat on the branch, as we
all climbed out of the water
to watch.

We held our breaths as he
scooted across the branch over the water.

Darlene Beck Jacobson

SNAP!

*The snap — CRACK — of that branch filled
the air like a gun shot, making
all of us suck in air
and shudder.*

*I knew Bill could swim, I'd
seen him do it many times. If
he'd gone into the water
feet first, I'd be
telling a different story.*

*I suspect the shock of
the branch giving way beneath him
didn't give him enough
time to prepare.*

*He went in the water
face down, cracking the side of his
head on the branch before he
went under.*

*I hate to say this, but
three of us took off and ran.
It doesn't change things
to name who. It's on
their consciences.*

*Kevin and I were left. After seconds
that seemed to last forever, Bill
still hadn't come
to the surface.*

*I have to get him, I said.
Kevin tried to stop me, saying,*

It was stupid to take the dare. I
didn't think he'd do it.

It was stupid to make the dare, I
shouted at him
as I dove in.

Bill struggled,
trying to free his swim trunks with one arm,
the other arm dangling by his side.
His trunks were
caught on a jagged, splintered branch.
He blew out a last breath
of air, going limp.

I grabbed him under the arms,
pulling him free, leaving a pair of
shredded trunks behind.

When we surfaced, Kevin
was gone.

Dad's story ends with one last sentence:

Do the right thing, not
the easy thing.

I already knew Dad was
a hero. I just
never imagined his
bravery began
when he was a boy
like me.

I flip through the
last pages of the notebook, looking

Darlene Beck Jacobson

for more. Wanting,
needing to know
what happened to Bill after
Dad pulled him out of the water.

The rest of the pages are blank.

GUYS

An after-breakfast swim before
we change back into our shorts,
pack up for home. This time
I'm sitting up front with Pops,
just us guys talking Yankees baseball.

Pops asks, Want to go to a game, just
you and me, before you leave?
Heck, yeah is what I say. I
feel like jumping
the way Katy does when she's
excited, but we're in the car, so
I do a little bounce instead.

One of Pops' customers gave him two tickets.
The only person he wants to
go to a game with is me.

Making plans for this
guys-together thing is like extra frosting on
your favorite cake.

Leave it to Mom to ruin the moment by
saying the four most dreaded words guys
enjoying summer can hear:
Back
to
school
shopping.

Darlene Beck Jacobson

NINE

Nine pairs of shoes that all look the
same shiny black,
but Katy insists are different and
none quite right for the first
day of kindergarten.

No one is going to
look at your feet, I say as I hold
the shoebox containing my own brown shoes.
Maybe it is a big deal for Katy,
starting school for the first time.

For me, it's an awful reminder that
summer is nearly over and we,
Mom, Katy, and me,
will be leaving Gran and Pops and Jill,
going back to our other life,
the one without them.

Did I really not
want to come here? Did I groan
complain
fuss about everything those first few weeks?

It shames me to think of it because
now I can't imagine going back home,
leaving behind the
Dad I found here.

I take a deep breath and whisper
the wish that pokes at me, the wish that
Fred can't hear.
I wish you were home, Dad.

QUIT

I'm a wizard with a crystal ball,
a ball that shows the future.

Except when I look in it,
all I see is what can go wrong.

The thing I hope to see,
Dad whole
unharmed
perfectly imperfect like
he was before he left,
is so much smaller than
the scary things I imagine every time
I make the wish in my head.

Is there a foolproof way
to wish Dad home?

I need to answer the question, the
last question about
what happened to Bill after
Dad pulled him out of the lake.

I need a Dad wish that I can live with,
one that will let me sleep
without having nightmares.

I need to figure out what Dad
is telling me, not realizing his
own son
would be reading his boyhood words, words
that maybe hold the answers
I've been looking for.

Darlene Beck Jacobson

LOOT

Two
L
O
N
G
hours later, my stomach
growling like a grumpy bear, we
carry out shopping bags
stuffed with all the loot a kid needs for school.

Even though Mom protested,
Pops emptied his wallet to pay for everything.
Besides shoes
socks
underwear,
there are two pants and shirts for me,
two dresses for Katy,
a Barbie lunch box that has Katy wanting to
put food in it already.

Why didn't you get a lunch box, Jack?
Guys my age brown bag it, I say.

A second shopping bag holds
pencils
sharpeners
notebooks
a 64 pack of crayons that has Katy
sniffing and squealing over the colors,
wanting me to read the names of each one.
Later, I tell her.

There's also enough chalk to draw a line on the

highway all the way home probably.

Katy wears her
patent leather black shoes in the car, sitting
up front with Gran and Pops,
both of them beaming at her,
their own miracle,
their one-of-a-kind treasure no wish or
money can buy.

Mom snaps a picture of me with
my nose pressed
between the pages of one of the notebooks.

I take a whiff,
the smell of school disguised as paper,
a good smell, even though I complain.

I've done a lot of
thinking today, but not about school.

You know how
when you're not even thinking
about something and
an idea
a good idea
maybe the best idea comes to you?

That's what I'm hoping
will happen to me.

Tomorrow I'm going to
talk to Mr. Belcher.

We're close, Dad, hang on.

Darlene Beck Jacobson

GUTS

When I hear the doorbell
I think I'm dreaming because I
never sleep so late that I miss breakfast. It
has to be late for somebody to be ringing
the bell.

I roll out of bed and run
to the door because
nobody else is awake. Passing the clock
on the wall, I realize
it's still early.

Opening the door with sleep-filled eyes,
I come face to face with Cody.
Sorry to wake you, but
I couldn't wait anymore. I need your help.

Jill's getting her
fishing gear and meeting us at the pond.
He shuffles his feet but holds his eyes steady,
hands in fists at his side.

It took a lot of guts to come here alone,
asking for help without Jill as a messenger.

We'll meet you in an hour at the pond.

Thanks, he says,
blowing a puff of air that makes his
shoulders slump,
not relief but more like determination to
see this through.

He gets on his bike, gives me a
small wave, and disappears
down the road.

Darlene Beck Jacobson

LUCK

It takes feet tickling to
wake up Katy from her dreamland.
Why are we up early? It's not a tent day, Katy says.

He came back, is all I have to say for Katy to
hop from bed and get dressed.

Is Cody the kind Cody or the bully Cody?
Can I have some Sugar Pops first?
Are you going to ask Fred for another wish?
Can I bring the kite?
Questions spill out of her like
sugar from those shakers at the diner.

Hush, I whisper, We don't want to wake
everyone up.
We are going to the pond to save
a friend, maybe two.

Is this part of the plan Daddy
wrote about in the book?

I think so, I say, because
I'm still not sure what
it all means.

Katy's eyes get wider and she
pulls out the shoe box from our shopping trip.
I'm wearing my new shoes because
they're lucky.
How do you know that? I ask

When I have them on, I feel like I did

when Fred made the pancake wish come true.

Like anything's possible? I ask.
Katy nods.

We can use all the luck we can get, I say
as she follows me into the kitchen.
We wolf down bowls of
cereal and split a banana before we
head out the door.

I leave a note saying
we've gone fishing.

POKE

They're eating apples, staring across the pond
when we ride up. The sun is barely
over the edge of the water, even birds
sleeping at this hour.
We park bikes, join them on the grass.

When I ask, How was your trip,
they both talk at once,
making it hard to hear what they say,
only a few words that poke through,
awful
hopeless
nasty.
When they stop for air at the same time, I ask,
Why are we here?

Jill speaks solo this time. For the whole car ride
we told Mom about the things
that happened since Dale came.

Mom kept shaking her head, mumbling no, no,
until I pulled off her sunglasses,
made her listen again as Cody told his story.

Did you tell her about the wishes? I ask.

Jill shakes her head. It was hard enough
getting her to believe
the rest without that, she says.

But she believes it? I ask.
Sort of. Jill sighs, pokes Cody in the
ribs with an elbow

because he isn't talking.

After a sigh he says, She thinks I need
counseling
medicine
maybe a doctor.
He tries not to show the hurt on his face.
You'd have to be blind not to see it.

What about your grandmother? I ask,
frustrated that now
that I can hear them, they need
a poke to get the words out.

Mom brought us there to ask a
different question.
Jill's eyes fill up with tears.

What question?

Her chin quivers as she says, Mom wanted
to know if Cody and me could
come and live with Nana
until Mom worked things out with Dale.

Katy stands up, stomps her feet,
hands on hips, yelling,
No, your mommy can't give you away!

Jill sighs, Nana said no, too,
which made Mom stop listening.

I'm here to ask you for help, Jack, Cody says.
Jill says you still have wishes.

Can I use one?

Darlene Beck Jacobson

HEAT

I feel heat rise from my chest
up my neck
to my face, burning so hard,
I can't keep my tongue still.

You had three wishes! I shout at Jill.
We agreed the last one was it.

The four eyes that stare back at me are
fearful
sad
worried.

Who do these two kids,
kids I didn't even know before this summer,
who do they think they are,
asking
begging
wanting another wish?

Why don't you catch Fred and
make your own wishes, I tell Cody,
staring him down
until he is the first to look away.

After a heavy sigh, the confession comes out.

I've been trying to do that all week.

KNOWLEDGE

Cody's shoulders slump as he says,
I came here to catch Fred,
to see if what you said about him is true.

Everyday I waited and waited,
ready to ask Fred for help.

I had no trouble catching him,
but every time I tried to make a wish,
he'd wiggle free.
Not once
or twice
five times for five days,
even with a net, he'd flip out and swim away.

Cody sighs, I must be a jinx or something.
Fred won't let me have any wishes.

Why? Katy asks.

Cody and Jill shrug.

With the shrug goes my anger
as I realize what's going on. If I had one
wish left
I'd run
get away
leave these two
to figure it out on their own. They
caused the whole mess.

But I'm in it too, for telling Jill about Fred.
I'm part of the mess. Two wishes.

Darlene Beck Jacobson

If I do it right, I'll only need one for Dad.

All of a sudden,
the snap
the crack of the branch, a
voice in my head, a voice that
sounds like Dad's, whispers
suggests
encourages
Do the right thing, not the easy thing.

That voice brings something else,
knowledge, sure and true.

The knowledge that sometimes
in order to help yourself,
you have to help
someone else first.

We're the ones who started wishing
for Cody, I tell Jill.
We have to be the ones who finish.

One wish only, I say.
It can't be any other way. Don't
mess this up.

Two heads bob up and down in relief.

LION

You need to be careful what you wish for
I say, or things could be even worse
than they are now.

Cody nods his head. I realize that
all the things that happened
aren't your fault or Jill's fault, he says.

I know I didn't have to be a bully, but
Dale made it hard not to be one. Everything
changed
when he came, so if he's gone…

I put up both hands. WHOA, I say,
shaking my head so hard I get dizzy.
You can't wish for Dale to disappear.
I say it loud, in his face,
so there is no doubt I mean business.

My dizziness gets worse
thinking of all the things that
could happen with that kind of wish.

The wish has to give somebody something, I say
not take away something. That's
the only way to stop weird things from happening.

I think so too, he says. So here's my wish.
I want to ask for courage,
to be brave and strong enough
to stand up to Dale.

I stare at Cody, standing tall,

looking hopeful, eyes pleading,
asking for the wish of the Cowardly Lion in the
Wizard of Oz, to have courage.

The same wish another boy made,
all those years ago.

Maybe wishes are really mirrors
that show us what's been there all along,
only we never pay attention.

I think of how much courage it took
to ask for help, to want to be better.

Cody's always been brave, he just needed to
lose himself a little,
in order to find his courage.

That's the wish you should make, I say.

JOAN

Not even trying or wanting to,
we catch so many fish with
Jill's pole, enough to fill a bucket,
wondering
hoping
praying
Fred is still in the pond, never dreaming
he might be gone.

I'm ready to go home, take a break,
plus I really
want
need to talk to Mr. Belcher.

One worm left, Jill says, handing
the pole to Cody. Maybe if
you put it on the hook
this time Fred will come.

Cody looks at me. I shrug. Do it, I say.

The bobber hits the water,
does a little dance and disappears.
Cody reels in the catch dangling from the hook.

It's Fred! yells Katy as I
hold out my net. Fred slides into it.
He winks his fish eye at me,
nudging
encouraging
waiting for a wish.

When Cody speaks

Darlene Beck Jacobson

something shifts, changes. He doesn't ask
for courage for himself as I expected,
he wishes courage and bravery
for someone named Joan.

Fred's fish eye
stops winking, stares as if
it can't believe — like me — what it sees, hears.

Fred blinks his fish eye at me, the one
who holds the wish.
Who's Joan? I whisper.

Our mother, Jill says as she and Cody lock eyes.

I hadn't thought of this.
Will it be a wish that goes wrong like
all the others?
Why did you change the wish? I ask.

Cody sighs. I realized my bravery
or Jill's bravery won't mean much
if Mom can't stand up to Dale on her own.

I look back at Fred. Courage for Joan, I say,
before Fred winks twice and slithers
back under the water.

SIGH

That's it? Cody asks.
That's it, I nod.

No bells, whistles, or beams of light
bursting from the sky,
nothing to let us know things
are different.

Only this deep, heavy sigh from Cody,
a sigh that makes him
stand taller, hold his head higher.

He shakes his arms and each leg,
like he's getting rid of
pests, flicking away
something unwelcome.

Then, what I've never seen before on this boy,
a real smile filling his face,
a face made different by giving someone else
his courage.

What now? I ask Cody and Jill.
Food, they say together while Katy cheers.
Then I have to make good on
a promise, Cody says
as he looks at Katy. We have a kite to fly.

I slip the bucket of fish
over the handlebars of my bike as we
ride to Gran's for lunch.

Darlene Beck Jacobson

OKAY

I don't even care that
we're having tuna sandwiches with
rainbow-colored vegetable sticks.

Cody hasn't stopped talking,
mostly to Katy, who listens to him as if he's
Mr. Wizard, the guy on TV who can
answer any question a kid asks.

Cody is now her official
brother, joining Jill in that club of
special people,
Katy's club where there is
always room for one more.

Jill stares at her brother
the way I sometimes stare at Katy, with
one part awe
one part mystery
and the biggest part love.

Even though the hard thing
still waits for Cody and Jill,
I know they will be okay
because the Cody Jill remembers
found his voice.

DEEP

When I enter the Sweet Shop
after lunch, Mr. Belcher
greets me, saying, Good afternoon, Jack.
Riding solo today?

Before he wonders or
ask questions grown-ups ask
when they talk to kids,
I take a deep breath and say
what I've rehearsed for days.

I tell him about the book, spilling out,
pouring out the story
Dad wrote before I lose
my nerve,
leaving out the
wishes and dares that
aren't for Mr. Belcher to know.

When I stop to
take a breath, before I get
a chance to ask
my question, Mr. Belcher says,
I didn't know you were
Todd's boy.

I should have known. You have the
same integrity
honor
determination he had.

When Todd pulled me
out of the lake,

out of the deep, when I was
sure I would
drown, he not only
saved my life, he
changed it forever.

LIFT

Your Dad jumped in
when no one else did. I
figured I was on
my own as soon as I went
out on that branch.

I went into the water a
fake
an imposter
a foolish boy
who pretended to be brave.

Todd lifted me out
lifted me up
gave me another chance. The
boy I was drowned in that lake.

I stare at Mr. Belcher as
he tells me this with
tears in his eyes.

Dad didn't write about
what happened after he pulled you
out, I say.

Mr. Belcher nods. I suppose
he figured it was my
story to tell.
He lifts his left arm with his
right hand, a useful hand helping the one
that dangles at his side.

I am reminded of that jump every day of

Darlene Beck Jacobson

my life. My injury caused
paralysis of the left arm. I had to learn to
write
open jars
do everything right-handed.
Took me awhile since I
was a lefty. But it was my fault. I am also
reminded
grateful
thrilled
to have a chance to do life over again.

He smiles at me. Thanks to your Dad.
Last I heard, he
had a career in the Army. Is he still serving
our country?

A POW in Vietnam, I say.

He shakes his head, the pain
in his face so real,
I feel it in mine.

If I remember anything about
your dad, I know
he's fighting. He may seem
quiet on the outside,
but inside, he's a
force to reckon with.

Don't you give up on him,
because he'd never give up
on himself or
anyone else.

I know that now, I say.

I sit quietly sipping the
ice cream soda Mr. Belcher
made for me, feeling a warm wave
of pride
sweep through me with
each sip.

Darlene Beck Jacobson

FOUR

Our last night in the tent,
four of us stuffed elbows to knees,
five if you count Bouncy who
still manages to show up, pig tape scars and all.

Sharing our best part of the weird summer
because
we already survived the worst part.
You first, Katy, I say.

Being five and having four new friends.
I only see two in this tent, I say.
Katy giggles. Silly Jack, you forgot Fred,
she says
in a hands-on-hips voice,
wondering how we could forget the fish.
Jill and Cody shout, Three cheers for Fred!

Number four?

The boy in Dad's book, Katy says.
It always amazes
dazzles
surprises me when
she says things like that.

Jill's turn, I say.
Having my brother back she says,
even though Cody is making a face pretending to gag.

Cody says, the best part was
everything that happened since Katy's
birthday and how

you all welcomed me, even when I wasn't
me. I don't know
if I would have found myself without that.

I shove him with an elbow, he shoves back.
Your turn, Jack, Cody says.

The best part for me is
knowing this isn't the end but a
different beginning.

Forever friends I say,
A team,
our own Fab Four.

We pile our hands
one on top of another, raising the
hand pile to the tent roof.

Darlene Beck Jacobson

DAWN

We wake up with the birds,
beating them to the worms we dig up
with sleep-filled eyes.

Gulping milk, grabbing fishing gear,
bananas, and a bag of Oreos,
heading to the pond as the sun rises,
dawn of a new day, a new beginning.

A wish I thought would
be solo, but realize it will be for all of us.

To make the wish, that last wish,
will close the door we opened without knowing
what lay on the other side.

Three poles in the water and still
it is the one I hold that brings Fred.

How does he know which
worm leads to me?

Cody holds the net as we
stare into the blinking eye of
our fish.

The one-eyed fish
who changed our lives.

LOVE

Fred gives his one-eyed wink, his sign
that means
this is it, boy, your last chance
to get it right. After this, we're done.

I take a deep breath, look at
my sister
my friends
as I say the wish I should have wished
from the beginning,
the one that might have saved us from
all the trouble.

A wish
a prayer
the best, most loving thing
I can do for Dad,
for everyone I love who is
part of this summer.

In a voice steady and clear, I say,
Keep Dad and all of us
safe.

Fred winks,
opens and closes his fish lips in a
goodbye kiss, before I send him back to the
sounds of thanks
gratitude
appreciation
for bringing two families together.

Darlene Beck Jacobson

SOAR

Turns out Cody is the king of kite flying.
He knows just how much
to run, letting out just enough string,
bits at a time, until a gust of wind
catches the silk, lifting it skyward.

As we watch it rise, Cody
hands the roll of string to Katy, showing her
how to tug the line
to keep the kite flying high.
A silk bird lifting,
soaring on the wind,
taking our spirits for a ride.

We all seem lighter,
as if our worries took off with the kite
scattering them across the fields like
dandelion fluff, making them
smaller
less bothersome
nearly invisible.

Has this last wish for bravery
spilled over, changed me somehow?

For now at least,
I am the kite.
Watch
me
soar.

TODD

Tomorrow Pops and I are
heading into the Big Apple for the
Yankee game against the Red Sox,
my first and second
favorite teams, so whoever wins is
okay by me.

In four days we head back home to
the house without Dad.

Mom brought us here, thinking it would
keep us busy, help us
stop missing Dad so much.

Instead, it feels
like we brought Dad with us to this place.

Everyday I've been here, it's like
Dad sat beside me, whispering in my ear.

Sleeping in his tent, riding his bike,
and going to the places he went when
he was a kid. Knowing
he went through the same
things I did.

Reading his words, hearing
his voice, helped me
figure out
how to use my last wish.

Tonight I'm reading Katy the
bedtime story she

264   *Darlene Beck Jacobson*

always wants,
like she can't hear it
enough. The story of a
boy named Todd.

TEAM

A day at the ballpark with Pops
and my two favorite teams feels like
a dream you never want to wake up from.

Four rows behind home plate,
the grass is so green it hurts my eyes.
So much noise, Pops and me
have to yell at each other to be heard.

Smell of hotdogs, warm and
dripping with mustard,
tastes better than any hotdog
I ever ate. Even the seats,
sticky with spilled soda and beer,
feel solid under me. Only one thing
would make this one-of-a-kind day better.

A team of three.

Where are you, Dad? Do you remember
our Little League team
that never won a game our first year?
That didn't stop us from playing hard, so hard
that the second season we were 6-6.
Team work.

Thinking about Jill and her family team
that may not win every game but are still a team, together.

Things work out better when
you work together, like we learned
in Little League.
Yankees beat the Red Sox, 9-3.

266

Darlene Beck Jacobson

CUTE

The birds in our box have hatched,
a squawking nest of
bald
scrawny
blind
alien creatures with mouths
wide open every time we
take a peek inside.

They're so cute!!! Katy gushes
when she sees them.

There are a lot of words I would use
to describe a just-hatched baby bird,
but cute is not one of them. Yet
when I look at them
thrusting their heads up,
trusting that food will follow,
it is kind of amazing that these
un-cute creatures will grow to be birds,
just like their parents.

Makes me think
about Gran and her miracle seeds.
There is something unreal
magical
maybe even
miraculous
about watching things grow.

HERO

When I was little, I always thought
a hero was a guy like Superman. A
tough guy who was never afraid.

But a hero doesn't have to be tough, and
plenty of heroes are scared. They fight
battles big and small. Dad and Pops
are heroes.
Everybody agrees with that.

Mom and Gran are heroes, too.

They keep families together when
things seem hopeless.
People who do brave things
even when they're scared are heroes.

I discover a bunch more as I watch
Cody and Jill stand next to
their mother Joan and their grandmother
who rode into town to join the
gang of hand-holding heroes,
watching as Dale starts up a moving van
we all helped load with
most of the things from Jill's house,
leaving behind the junkiest car
and a few crummy pieces of furniture.

The van is barely down the road before
shouts
cheers
songs fill the air.

Darlene Beck Jacobson

Joan throws her sunglasses to the sidewalk,
steps on them and invites all of us
to do the same, as the last reminder
of a foolish mistake is ground into plastic bits that
blow away in the wind.

LEFT

We never went roller skating, says Katy.
And I didn't go to a carnival or learn to play badminton,
Jill adds.

We're
telling Cody about the things we did
before he was part of us.

It's good to have some things left, he says.
That will give us stuff to do
when we get together next summer.

What about the banana split? Katy jumps
up and down,
landing on the grass in a
perfect split of her own as we cheer and clap.
There's ice cream left from the party and Gran
always has bananas, I say.

Last one in has to growl like a bear, I say.
Snort like a pig, Jill adds
While flapping their arms like
a buck, buck chicken, says Cody.

The three of us
Jack
Jill
Cody
do those things, taking our time
as Katy cartwheels across the backyard,
beating us into the house.

Darlene Beck Jacobson

HAND

It's Jill's idea to trace everyone's hand,
both hands actually, so we can make two circles
with hands joined together, fingers
touching wrists,
so it looks like a paper wreath.

Hands of friendship, Jill says, Forever linked.
And holding on to hope, I say, thinking of Dad.

We trace the grown-ups' hands too,
all of us linked together
in a circle that doesn't end, like the silly song.

Jill and Cody keep one circle,
and I give the other to Gran and Pops.
We have to make another one, Katy says.
I want a hand wreath so I can always remember
my summer of wishes and how all of them
came true.

Eyes wide, Katy says, Let's write a wish
on each one so
next year we can see if they
come true without Fred.

Kid genius, Cody says, smiling at Katy.

I think we should keep them
secret, I say as we write down our
hopes and dreams on this third wreath.

We cover the back of each hand with
a paper door,

to be opened like a time capsule
next time we meet. We trade this new one,
the one with our
hopes and dreams,
for the one we gave Gran and Pops,
so we aren't tempted to take a peek.

Darlene Beck Jacobson

YEAR

We promise to write letters,
send postcards from places we visit, be
pen pals until
we see each other again next summer,
a whole year away.

Katy has a hard time,
saying goodbye to Jill and Cody through tears.
A year is forever
when you're five.

Feels like we just got here,
now we're leaving Gran and Pops behind.
Will there ever
be a time when everyone I love will be
together in the same place?

Gran bakes sugar cookies shaped like fish,
Fred cookies Katy calls them,
for our road trip home. We munch them
in the car, thinking our own thoughts
making our own plans
wondering what lies ahead
for each of us.

There is one thing I'm happy
to leave behind. My
worry about Dad.

Wherever he is,
he's safe.

SAFE

Dad,
After a summer like this, I feel
like I could take on the world
do anything
even stand up to
resident bully Chip McClosky
when I get back to school.

Maybe the wishes were only coincidences
or windows that showed us what was
already there. Or maybe they
just gave us the courage to
be our best selves. No matter.

I can't wait until
you get home, Dad, so I can
tell you all about
a fish
a wish
and how to stand up to a bully.

Better yet, you can
read it all, just as I wrote it for you.

Then you'll know you
haven't missed anything because
you're there, Dad, on every page.

I know you'll be back,
because Mom, Katy, Gran, Pops
and me, all of us are
holding on to hope. And
Fred,

Darlene Beck Jacobson

that fish I mentioned,
granted my wish.

Love,
your son,
Jack.

Author's Note

When I visit schools and talk to children, I am often asked where do you get an idea for a story. Ideas are everywhere, I tell them and this story is a wonderful example.

The idea for *Wishes, Dares, & How to Stand Up to a Bully* came to me in a dream, or rather the twilight between dreaming and full wakefulness, that moment when you're not quite ready to jump out of bed. I am not a person who usually remembers dreams. It frustrates me that no matter how often I try to pull at the threads of a pleasant dream, they drift away like so much dandelion fluff.

On one particular morning in early June 2018, I awoke with the name JACK and a number of four letter words circling around my thoughts like a mantra. The more these words circled, the more they took shape and began shouting at me. "Here's the title!" "Here's the premise…of a boy missing his father who is at war." "This is how you're going to write Jack's story — in free verse!" I repeated these words, phrases, titles, like a song I wanted to memorize so I wouldn't forget.

Before I headed to the shower, before I ate, before I did anything in my normal morning routine, I raced out of bed, grabbed a notebook and pencil, and wrote down everything circling in my brain. Pages and pages filled the notebook, including a list of four letter words I hoped to use in the story. Several pages later, when I felt relief that I hadn't lost this dream — this gift every writer hopes for – I breathed a sigh and began my day.

Out of all the manuscripts I've ever written, none has been more joyful to write. I met Jack each day with a new word. He told me his story and I wrote it down, just as he spoke it. The muse from my dream was the voice of an eleven year old boy. I hope you enjoy the result.

Notes Regarding the Setting

When Jack began telling me his story, I wasn't sure when and where it was taking place. As I got further into it, and his sister Katy and new friend Jill became larger and more fleshed out, I knew the story had to be during a more "innocent" — yet still modern — era of the past. No cell phones or electronic gadgets, no worry about kids being out all day unsupervised. A time when it was okay to be out riding bikes, playing, fishing, and hanging out without adults nearby. But also a time where exciting new things were on the horizon. Polio vaccines, Instamatic cameras, color television, were a few examples of the latest technology. The early sixties – the era that I grew up in — fit that criteria.

Manned space flight, with the goal of landing a man on the moon before the decade's end, was one of the hallmarks of the Kennedy Administration. Students nation-wide watched, on black and white TVs, astronauts blasting into space as part of the science curriculum.

Make no mistake, it wasn't an era without fear or worry. It was the dawn of the Nuclear Age and we were waging a Cold War with the Soviet Union. In October of 1962, our country spent a tense and scary thirteen days on the brink of a nuclear war with Cuba and the Soviet Union. Soviet missiles based in Cuba were pointed at the US during this tense period known as the Cuban Missile Crisis. The crisis ended when President Kennedy agreed not to invade Cuba and Soviet Premier Krushchev agreed to remove the missiles. Still, students across the country practiced civil defense "duck and cover" drills, hiding under desks or up against the walls of the hallways. These drills were supposed to prepare us for whatever the Communists sent our way.

The assassination of President John F. Kennedy was a moment that defined a generation. Everyone old enough to remember that day —

November 22, 1963 – knew exactly where they were and what they were doing when they heard the news that our beloved president had been shot. It was the Baby Boomer generation's 9-11 moment.

Erupting from under the surface of society was racial unrest. The southern states were still following Jim Crow laws with segregation the law of the land. By the end of the decade, protests – both peaceful and violent – ushered in the Civil Rights Movement and the end of segregation.

The voices of women protesting for equal rights with men was another prominent social movement of the era.

It was also a time of an explosion in pop music thanks to bands like the Beatles who led the surge of musicians from England known as The British Invasion. The music, clothing, and vocabulary of these groups became part of American pop culture throughout the decade and beyond.

While most people associate the Vietnam War with the late sixties and early seventies, it was a conflict that began in 1955 and ended in 1975. The US involvement in South Vietnam changed over the course of the war but lasted a long 20 years. Most of the POW's held in Vietnam were officers like Jack's dad, rather than enlisted men. The late US Senator John McCain was a POW survivor of the war.

Song

This is the song that doesn't end
It just goes on and on my friend
Some people started singing it not knowing what it was
And they'll continue singing it forever just because
This is the song that doesn't end.

Listen to the Lamb Chop version of the song from the Shari Lewis show:
https://youtu.be/HNTxr2NJHa0

Acknowledgements

As quick and effortless as this story seemed to be, there are still many people whose insight, attention to detail, and kind, thoughtful suggestions made it so much better. When I was only a dozen poems or so into the story, fellow writers Johanna Staton and Marina Cohen heard the early entries at an impromptu sharing session hosted by Marina at her house in the suburbs of Toronto. Their enthusiasm and encouragement for the free-verse format made me feel I might have an idea worth pursuing. Thanks, my writer friends, for that much-needed positive energy.

Huge thanks to the beta readers whose insight went a long way toward fine-tuning Jack's voice and the story arc. Dianne Salerni, Holly Schindler, Malayna Evans, Marilyn Ostermiller, and Joshua David Bellin – your suggestions, feedback, and insights were just what I needed to ground the story and conflict and keep everything moving in the right direction. Thanks especially to Dianne for the Monkey's Paw reference. I needed a "cautionary tale" to keep Jack from making a big mistake. Thanks to my daughter Amanda for feedback on early drafts, my son Erik for cheering me on, and my husband Jake for giving me the quiet time I need to write. Your joy in my successes means the world to me.

I am indebted, as always, to my super agent Liza Fleissig who remained open minded about the story even after I told her it was "a middle-grade historical fiction in free verse with an element of magical realism." I know she's shaking her head reading this, since many other agents might have said, "No. Way."

My biggest appreciation goes to my editor, author, illustrator, and a super hero of the publishing world, Marissa Moss from Creston Books. Her enthusiasm and love of Jack's story from the beginning assured me that she would help make it the best it could be. She finds things I miss and provides the "tough love" needed to get the story right. Thanks for helping me sweat out every detail to get all the pieces correct.

I tried to be as faithful and accurate to the time period as possible. Any errors are not Jack's fault, but my own.

Darlene Beck Jacobson
March 2019

Bibliography

Burns, Ken, and Novick, Lynn, directors. *The Vietnam War*. PBS, 2017.

Ostler, Rosemarie. *Dewdroppers, Waldos, And Slackers: A Decade-By-Decade Guide To The Vanishing Vocabulary Of The 20th Century*. Oxford University Press, 2003, pp. 119-143.

https://www.history.com/topics/cold-war/cuban-missile-crisis

http://www.baseball-almanac.com/teamstats/schedule.php?y=1964&t=NYA

About the Author

Darlene Beck Jacobson has a BA in Special Education and a Reading Specialist MA. She worked as a Speech Language Specialist with the Glassboro Public Schools in Glassboro, New Jersey for twenty years. Her first book, the award-winning *Wheels of Change,* came out with Creston Books in 2014. When not writing, Darlene substitute-teaches in her former school district. You can read more about her at www.darlenebeckjacobson.com.